ALSO BY GABE ROTTER

Duck Duck Wally

THE HUMAN
BOBBY

GABE ROTTER

SIMON & SCHUSTER PAPERBACKS
New York   London   Toronto   Sydney

Simon & Schuster Paperbacks
A Division of Simon & Schuster, Inc.
1230 Avenue of the Americas
New York, NY 10020

First Simon & Schuster trade paperback edition August 2010

SIMON & SCHUSTER PAPERBACKS and colophon are
registered trademarks of Simon & Schuster, Inc.

For information about special discounts for bulk purchases,
please contact Simon & Schuster Special Sales at
1-866-506-1949 or business@simonandschuster.com.

The Simon & Schuster Speakers Bureau can bring authors
to your live event. For more information or to book an event,
contact the Simon & Schuster Speakers Bureau at
1-866-248-3049 or visit our website at www.simonspeakers.com.

Designed by Esther Paradelo

Manufactured in the United States of America

10   9   8   7   6   5   4   3   2   1

Library of Congress Cataloging-in-Publication Data
Rotter, Gabe.
   The human bobby : a novel / Gabe Rotter.
      p.   cm.
   1. Physicians—Fiction. 2. Married men—Fiction. 3. Fathers—Fiction.
4. Successful people—Fiction. 5. Life change events—Fiction. 6. Homeless
men—Fiction. 7. Kidnapping—Fiction. 8. California, Southern—Fiction.
I. Title.
   PS3618.O869H86 2010
   813'.6—dc22   2010004237

ISBN 978-1-4391-6811-0
ISBN 978-1-4391-6814-1 (ebook)

This one is for the baby in the belly.
I love you so much already.

losing love is like a window in your heart,
everybody sees you're blown apart.

—*Paul Simon*

THE HUMAN BOBBY

CHAPTER
Thirty-one

There's a staccato *clicking* sound in my head.

Like a troupe of tiny, uncoordinated tap dancers performing on my brain.

The choppy, aggravating CLICK-clack-CLICK is interrupted when Eddie says "First I'ma find that fucker Manny and I'ma grab him by his greasy hair and BASH BASH BASH his fuckin' head against the sidewalk till I can feel his squishy brains oozing through my fingers . . . then I'm thinkin' Burger King."

Eddie's crazy.

I look at him, bewildered and cautious. "Huh?"

"You assed me what I'm up to today, Doc."

I rub my head. "No . . . I didn't."

"Yeah, Doc! You just did!"

"Okay, okay," I say, trying to temper his agitation, which tends to flare up with little provocation. This little shit named Manny Pedí had fucked us over pretty badly a few days prior, and Eddie was still on the warpath. "Maybe I'll join you for the Burger King portion of that itinerary, Eddie."

"Done dealio, Doc," says Eddie, with nice consonance and a smack on my shoulder. My name is Bobby. Flopkowski. But no one has called me that in a long time. Everyone out here just calls me Doc, and that's because I'm a doctor. Or, I *was* a doctor. A long time ago. In my last life.

I *was* a lot of things.

I was a husband. I was a father. I was happy.

I don't like to think about it.

"You know, Doc," Eddie continues, scratching his chin, some sure-to-be-peculiar notion percolating. "Check this out." *Here we go,* I thought. "Okay. The word 'homeless' is fuckin' bullshit, right? I mean, yeah, we don't have a home. Okay. Fine. I *git* that. Whateva. Okay? But—here—look at this." Eddie fishes around for something in the deep front pocket of his long, dingy overcoat, and I watch him, wondering where this is going, glad, at least, that he'd moved on from the Manny rage.

To call Eddie and I complete opposites would not be an exaggeration. Eddie is an enormous beast of a man. He's got to be almost seven feet tall, and I figure he topples the scales at about 350. He has dark brown skin as rough and tough as sequoia bark, and a shaved head like a wrecking ball. His muscles look like they were sculpted out of stone. He's got a gnarled scar that runs like railroad tracks on a raised relief map, from the corner of his right eye to the corner of his mouth on the same side, which he sustained in a knife fight when he was ten years old. They call him "Coastal Eddie" because he won't go more than a few blocks away from the beach. He has his reasons, and he doesn't discuss them. He's the toughest, strongest, scariest man I've ever known, and he's my best friend in the world and my protector. Me, I'm a fairly diminutive white guy, and although I'm certainly much tougher than I once was, I don't hold a candle to Eddie. No one does.

Eventually Eddie pulls out a pack of gum from his bottomless pocket. He holds it up for me and points to the tiny writing on the side, his finger twice the thickness of the little green package. "Sugar-*freeeee*. Okay? See where I'm going wit this, Doc?"

"Mmmm, no."

"Says sugar-FREE. Not sugar-LESS. It's *free* of sugar, right? *No sugar*. Sugar-*less* has *less* sugar, right? And, it's not like we have *less* of a home! We have *no* fuckin' home! Okay? None! Right? So I'd really, like, appreciate it if people would start calling us 'home*free*' instead of 'home-*less*.' You wit me, Doc?"

I suck some air through my teeth and make a doubtful clicking sound out of the corner of my mouth. It's my job to poke holes in Eddie's various ramblings and postulations while walking the very fine line between breezy conversational Eddie and I-might-snap-and-rip-your-face-off-your-head Eddie.

"What, Doc? What's the problem?"

I get a lot more slack with Eddie than anyone else seems to get. I think maybe it's because I'm a doctor. But more likely it's because I saved his life once. I like these conversations because when Eddie talks to me the clicking noise in my head seems to disappear.

"Well, shoot, Eddie, that doesn't really hold up, man."

"Whaddaya mean, Doc?"

"I mean, look, the word 'less,' when used at the end of a word, means 'without.' Not 'a smaller amount of.'"

"Nah, Doc. Less! It means . . . you know, *less*."

"Not in that case, Eddie. And sugarless gum has no sugar."

"Nah."

"Eddie—I'm telling you, bud. Yes."

Eddie stops and thinks. He scratches his scruffy chin some more. You might think Eddie was dumb upon first meeting him. Men of his monstrous size tend to give that impression. But Eddie's not dumb at all. In fact, in my time with him, he's made some brilliant, keen observations about life that completely dropped my jaw. This, however, isn't one of those moments.

Finally he says, "Prove it, Doc."

"Okay, well . . . 'worthless' means 'without worth.' 'Hopeless'—without hope. Speechless! 'Without words.'"

Eddie sort of nods his head and smiles a bit. "Damn, Doc. You good."

"And anyway, Eddie, 'home free' doesn't exactly sum up our lives too accurately."

"Aw hell, Doc," says Eddie with a flourish of his thick hand. "This ain't so bad."

We sit there in silence for a while, watching the sunrise over the Pacific Ocean. Hearing the sounds. Smelling the smells. Two homeless guys, enjoying the morning.

I have to admit, Eddie was right. Not about the sugarless gum thing, of course, but that most of the time, being homeless here in Santa Monica isn't so bad. The cops don't harass the non-drugging/non-drinking/non-crazy guys like us. It rarely rains. Up until a few days ago and the whole Manny debacle, we had a pretty nifty four-man tent that we set up each night—usually on the beach—to house the two of us and our assorted gear. We've worked out deals with a few of the finer eating establishments in the area, whereby they give us leftover food that would normally go in the Dumpster in exchange for us making sure that no vagrants beg/sleep/defecate/urinate outside of their restaurants. Sometimes I even give free medical advice to the busboys and dishwashers. Everybody wins. Heck, I probably eat at the Ivy more than some Hollywood starlets. I get mine to go.

We actually don't even look like homeless guys. We wash our clothes often. We shower daily down by the beach where most people just wash the sand off their feet. I'm much thinner than I was when I was a normal denizen of society, and my beard is longer and grayer, but aside from that, I don't think you'd know I was homeless unless I told you so. What I'm trying to say is, I'm not one of these homeless wack jobs, running around in my own filth talking to myself or screaming at the sky. Trust me, I know wack jobs. My father, though he wasn't homeless, was pretty much off his rocker, so I'm pretty sensitive about avoiding that fate at all costs.

I'm just a normal guy. With no home.

Of course, walking the streets as what amounts to a vagabond, you can't help but sometimes feel like a flea on a bald head; it's hard to blend in.

Before they were destroyed by Manny, all of my worldly possessions fit into one small suitcase on wheels. Several changes of clean clothes, a toiletry kit (toothbrush/paste, soap, shampoo, deodorant, sunscreen), several books, a top-notch first aid kit, a Leatherman tool, a bottle for water, a flashlight, a lighter, two towels (which are the most useful things in my case—as I learned from Douglas Adams—a towel can be used as a washcloth, a pillow, a blanket, a napkin, a handkerchief, a place mat, to sit on, lie on, stand on, sleep on, filter water through, as an extra layer for warmth, a bandage, or a tourniquet. I could use it for shade, to carry things, to wrap things in for safety. I could put a rock in it and use it as a weapon. Mostly, though, I just used it to dry myself off). I also had a great sleeping bag that was given to me by an old friend, the same one who gave me the tent. And finally, the most important of my possessions: a small blue stuffed bear that I gave to my son on the day he was born (that I swear still smells like him), and a manuscript for a novel that was written by my father. Oh, and a gun (we'll get to that later). These things were all I had, and they were all I needed. There is a quote by the Roman philosopher Seneca that goes, "What difference does it make how much you have? What you do not have amounts to much more." That's my accidental and undesired credo.

I've learned to live like this, over the years. Better put, I've learned to *survive* like this. Do I miss having a home? Sure I do. Nowadays more than ever. I miss the smell of my house. I miss having a refrigerator full of food. I miss waking up in a bed. I miss the doorbell ringing. I miss watching TV on the couch with my feet up on the ottoman. I miss strolling through the house at night to turn all the lights off. I miss the feeling of *homeness.* But these are all things I've managed to live without. A vital part of me died when I lost my wife and my child. The part that worried. The part that loved. The part that needed life's little luxuries. My life is simple now, for better or worse.

At least that's what I would have said before this morning.

It started out like most days. Eddie and I woke up, watched the sun rise, and hiked up to the Pacific Palisades, a few miles from Santa Monica. Well, *I* went to the Palisades. Eddie, giving credence to his nickname, stayed on the beach. He was pretty agitated all morning about Manny. I needed to get away for a while.

This small group of black, crow-like birds had been circling above us since we'd awakened, incessantly swooping and caw-caw-cawing. Eddie was on edge, mumbling that the birds were an omen, a harbinger of bad things to come. I don't believe in omens, and I'd thought the worst had already come for me, but I was shaken up by the events of a few days ago, so the crows sort of freaked me out, too.

As I walked up from the beach to the Palisades, the *clicking* in my head returned. I tried to ignore it by whistling a song. Sometimes that works. I looked up and whistled and watched the birds circling. They were so high in the sky that they looked more like flies. I started to get dizzy so I had to look back down at the road. I saw something quick and small and dark skitter across my path and into some brush. I walked and whistled and tried to ignore the CLICK-clack-CLICKING that reverberated in between my ears.

I'd recently made friends with a café owner in Palisades Village who'd been giving me free breakfast every day out of the goodness of her heart. Her name is Cecilia. She has long silver hair, remarkably flawless skin for a woman of her age, blue eyes, and always a fresh flower behind her ear. She's one of the kindest, most genuine people I've ever met. Her café is called Café Emily, named after her only daughter. Cecilia sits and chats with me. She is fascinated by my stories. She tells me about her life as a surfer girl in the mid-'70s in Malibu. We are like old friends.

We chatted today. After all the craziness of a few days ago, I was pleased for the company. I was halfway through my scrambled eggs, telling her about what Manny had done and what he'd said, when I saw someone cross the street; someone who caught my eye.

Made me do a double take.

Stop talking.

Drop my fork.

Someone who would change absolutely *everything*.

CHAPTER
One

A va and I met at a bar mitzvah in 1990, on the dance floor, during the song "Gonna Make You Sweat (Everybody Dance Now)" by C+C Music Factory. I was twenty-eight, in med school, and fully adorned in party swag: a plastic yellow bowler hat, a green plastic lei, and neon-armed sunglasses. She was twenty-six, a waitress at a nightclub, and wearing green, purple, yellow, and black plastic leis, the same neon-sided sunglasses (hers had hot-pink arms, mine had green), and she was playing an inflatable plastic saxophone, though there was no saxophone nor any other instrument in the song. I was there with my girlfriend of the time (an immature, bumptious spoiled brat whom I was no longer into and wasn't sure why I'd ever been in the first place), who was best friends with the older sister of the bar mitzvah boy (well, I suppose he was technically a man by that point in the celebration), and Ava was there with her boyfriend, who was the older brother of said boy-man. Her boyfriend and my girlfriend were doing shots at the bar, which left Ava and me all by our lonesome.

Being that we were the only two in our demographic on the entire dance floor (everyone else either thirteen or fifty-five), we naturally gravitated toward each other. That's the official story, anyway. The truth is, I was sitting at a table by myself, downing vodka sodas, ready to go home, when I spotted her dancing with a crowd of horny thirteen-year-olds. When I say she was dancing with them, what I mean is, she was dancing and they were swarming her like bees at the hive, practically humping her legs. I wasn't much of a dancer, but when I saw her, I forgot all about that. I awkwardly boogied my way in her direction, decorating myself en route with the obligatory bar mitzvah dance floor peacockery, and we locked eyes. Without words, we flirted. I mocked her for dancing with the boys, and then began dancing with the thirteen-year-old girls. This went on for several minutes, each of us pretending to bask in the attention of our young groupies, in an unspoken competition for who could garner the bigger fan club. Finally, the boys began to grow more aggressive as the rapper in the song threatened to "make us sweat till we bleeeeeed," and she signaled to me with her eyes that she could use a rescue. I grabbed a plastic lei from a dancer, lassoed her, and reeled her in.

"Thank you, Superman," were the first words she ever spoke to me, as the song changed to "Pump Up the Jam" by Technotronic.

"Ahem, didn't you see the glasses?" I asked, intending to make a Clark Kent joke.

"What?" she shouted over the music, dancing way better than I ever could.

"I said, I'M CLARK KENT!" I wiggled the neon-armed glasses to try to emphasize my point, but the music was very, very loud.

"WHAT?" She was smiling and doing the Running Man and I didn't care that my extemporaneous little joke didn't work. I was smitten.

We danced and flirted and laughed for one more song ("Poison," Bel Biv DeVoe), but were rudely interrupted by her big, ugly, drunken boyfriend when the song "Nothing Compares 2 U" by Sinéad O'Connor came on. The wobbly jerkoff wanted his girlfriend back for the slow dance, and so it was back to my annoying girlfriend and my vodka sodas. As I stepped away I caught a glimpse of disappointment on Ava's face. At least that's what I told myself.

When I returned to my table, my girlfriend immediately started gossiping into my ear, and I pretended to listen, but I couldn't keep my eyes off of Ava. She had the most amazing blue eyes and wheat-colored, stick-straight hair. I remember admiring how remarkably clean and shiny it looked. Like straight out of a shampoo commercial. I knew it must smell like strawberries or some other mouthwatering, fruity thing. I soon caught her stealing glances at me in return. Her boyfriend was *very* drunk. He was hanging all over her, and he kept trying to dip her and spin her and she wasn't enjoying herself. And then it happened—the thing that changed the course of the rest of my life:

He vomited on the dance floor.

I couldn't have planned it better if I'd spiked his glass with ipecac. (I swear I didn't.) It was terrific. She was hit with some shrapnel from his puke explosion, and so while he was rushed to the bathroom, much to my girlfriend's chagrin, I moved in with some (vodka) soda water and a napkin.

"You guys were like Ginger Rogers and Fred Astaire out there. What happened?" I asked her as I wiped her dress with the wet cloth.

"Yeah, more like Ginger Rogers and Fred A-barf," she snarled.

"Oof. That was a *terrible* joke," I said with a smile, pulling back the napkin from her dress as if I were horrified.

"Dude, I just got vommed on. Maybe my sense of humor would be sharper if I weren't slathered in blown chunks." She grabbed my hand that held the napkin and said, "Dab, don't rub." I swear I felt electricity course through my body.

"You been firin' off jokes like that all night? Fred A-barf? I think I just figured out what made him sick."

She slapped my knee playfully. We were quiet for a moment while I dabbed away at the brown orange flecks on her dress. I could feel my girlfriend shooting eye-daggers at me. I didn't give a shit. "Thanks for cleaning me up," she eventually said. "Doug would *never* do that."

"It's my pleasure. Consider it retribution for not laughing at my dancing."

"Who said I wasn't laughing at your dancing?"

"Oh." I curled my lower lip and gave her my best sad face.

"Sorry. Your dancing needs a li'l work," she said with a cute smile.

"Least *my* dancing didn't make anyone throw up," I retorted.

She slapped me playfully again, harder this time, and formed her mouth into a mock-offended O shape.

"So—Doug—he's your boyfriend?" I asked, changing the subject, looking down at her stained dress and nervously scrubbing a bit harder than I probably needed to.

"Yeah, kinda," she said, sounding disappointed. "I'm pretty over him."

I could relate. This was my opportunity. I stood up and extended my hand. "I'm Bobby."

She smiled and rose, almost to my height. "I'm Ava."

"Pleasure to meet you, Ava."

"Likewise, Bobby."

"When you dump Fred A-barf, maybe you'd like to go out sometime?"

"I would like that very much. Maybe dance lessons?"

"Maybe dance lessons," I conceded.

We were married four years later.

CHAPTER
Two

I don't want to spew a saccharine, cloying fairy tale, but our life was pretty perfect for a long time. We got married right after I graduated from USC med school, had a small wedding at a restaurant in the valley, and settled into a little studio apartment in the Silver Lake area while I did my residency at a nearby hospital. Ava got a job as a hostess at a local restaurant that served a strange mix of Indian food and haute French cuisine. Most nights we ate whatever she could bring home. We didn't have a lot of money those first few years, and we were both working like dogs, but somehow it was okay. It was better than okay. Ava was the only family I'd had in a long time. Both of my folks died when I was pretty young, so I was anxious to start a family of my own, and Ava was, too. As corny as it may sound, we were so stupidly in love that at the end of each gruesome day, once we were together, we forgot about everything else, and we were happy.

When I think about that time in my life, it all blends into one warm, comfortable, safe blanket of memories. Sure, life was a bit of a struggle, but we were always raising our glasses and toasting to how damned lucky we were. Ava had this one toast she always said: "May our only pain be champagne." That was Ava in a nutshell back then; so positive, so full of good cheer and optimism. Or maybe I'm just looking back through rose-colored glasses. I don't know. It seems to me now that everything was as uncomplicated and sublime as a champagne toast.

Life took on a fairly pleasant cadence, and before I knew it, my residency was finished. I was fortunate enough during my three-year stint to befriend a fellow resident named Richard Sapp—"Dicky" to everyone who knew him for more than five minutes. Six foot four, perma-tan, great teeth, athletic build, and the angular, sharp-featured face and flawlessly side-slicked hair of a '50s movie star. Dicky was a total stud. The life of the party. A smart, boisterous (okay—obnoxious), handsome, super-spoiled rich kid from Bel-Air whose father was the head cardiothoracic surgeon at Cedars-Sinai Medical Center in Beverly Hills. You have to be pretty confident to pull off a nickname like "Dicky." When I asked him once why he didn't do his residency at his father's hospital instead of at the decidedly less spectacular Silver Lake General where we were stuck, he said that he didn't want to be given any advantages over anyone else. This, as he drove me home in the $100,000

Porsche Turbo his dad bought him when he got into med school.

Dicky and I were . . . different. In contrast to his *GQ* good looks and thick wallet, I was poor, not particularly tall, pale, and good-but-not-great-looking. He was loud, I was low-key. He was a partier, I was a studier. On paper we shouldn't have been friends. If I wasn't so giddily satisfied with my life at that time I probably would have been insanely jealous of him. Thing is, I was leaps and bounds smarter, and so he liked to stick by me because I was the sharpest one in our group, and also the least nerdy, aside from him. The only thing we had in common was that we both wanted to go into pediatrics. For me, it wasn't so bad being best buds with a guy like Dicky. Just by virtue of being near him I had access to things I'd never been exposed to before: vacations, lavish parties, beautiful women (though I never dabbled, it didn't hurt to *look*), nice cars, big houses. He was a magnet for these things. Not to mention he was a loyal friend and a pretty damned good doctor.

A few weeks before we finished our residency, I was sitting in the hospital cafeteria, halfway through a truly appalling plate of "meat loaf" and "mashed potatoes," when I saw Dicky galloping toward me with a goofy smile.

"Dr. Floppy!" (That's what Dicky called me back then. Very professional, and also very clever.) "Dude! Wait till you hear this shit!" he said as he plopped down across from me. "Ready? So I've been talking to my father about where to go from here."

"Uh-huh?" I said as I powered down some impossibly dry meat loaf.

"Yeah, dude. And he made me an offer I couldn't refuse."

"Oh yeah?" I said, finally able to swallow. "Was Luca Brasi there?"

"Funny. No—"

"Lemme guess. You're gonna go work at Cedars?"

"No, dude. Pff. Much better than that," he said, a smile smeared all over his face like cake frosting on the cheeks of a child. I thought he was going to say something ridiculous, like his father chose him to head up the new pediatric wing he was going to build at our hospital or something.

"Okay, you going to tell me? Or can I get back to my meat loaf?"

He looked at my food and shivered. "Listen—two words, motherfucker: Private. Motherfucking. Practice."

"That's three, arguably four words, but wow! That's great!" I reached over the table and held my fist out so he could give it a bump. "Which practice?" If you join the right one, private practice is a great way to make money and live a somewhat normal life as a doctor. I was sure with his father's connections, he'd be joining the right one.

"No, no. Not joining one, Floppy. *Starting* one. My dad is funding it. One of the older docs at his hospital, this guy Tobias Stenzler, is gonna go in with me. And guess what, fucker? I told them you're the best doctor in our group and they want you to come along, too!"

"Me?! Are you serious?" I almost choked on an especially rocky bite of mashed potato.

"Does the pope shit in the woods?"

"Private practice?!"

"Our *own* private pediatric practice," he said, while making the "moolah" sign with his fingers. "Get this, Flop: we'll pay you a hundred fifty grand the first year, plus a piece of every patient." He smiled big, and raised his hands, palms up. "Whaddaya think?"

"A hundred fif—what do I *think*?" I asked, my smile so big it was starting to hurt my face. We high-fived and hugged and jumped up and down and I nearly had to go to the restroom to vomit up my meat loaf.

And so it went. A few months later we opened up shop in a nice office in Brentwood, replete with a fish tank and real plants in the waiting room. Great location, wealthy clientele. Business picked up quickly and soon we were making good money. *Very* good money. Ava was able to quit her job, and we moved out of our crappy studio and bought a pretty nice little two-bedroom house in West Hollywood. We started to feel like a real married couple. Like grown-ups!

CHAPTER
Three

By 1998, thanks to a write-up in *Los Angeles* maga-zine's Best of L.A. issue, business was booming. Dicky had been cited in the article as one of the "Hot-test Bachelors in the City," and from that moment on, we couldn't curtail the flood of patients pouring into our office. Every hot little mama on the Westside and her runny-nosed two-year-old wanted an appointment with the studly Dr. Sapp. I played good cop to his stud cop—the friendly doctor everyone referred to simply as "Dr. Bobby." Mostly, he handled horny mommies, and I handled worried daddies. Or, as Dicky loved to put it in his patently brash way: "I handle the hotties with tykes, you handle the daddies and dykes." We were a good fit.

Ava and I had already moved out of our little house in West Hollywood to bigger digs in Beverly Hills. The new house was a dream come true: five bedrooms, a gym, big country kitchen, a billiards room, hot tub, built-in BBQ, three-car garage, and a half basketball court. Not bad for a poor kid from Brooklyn.

We fell into a routine at home. I woke up early every day, ate breakfast with Ava, went to the office for eight, nine, sometimes ten, eleven hours, came home, ate dinner with Ava, and went to bed. Ava, now jobless, had been spending most of her time designing and decorating our new home. We spent the weekends together, mostly at places like Pottery Barn or Crate and Barrel. I watched football on Sundays. She took cooking classes on Tuesdays and Thursdays, pottery classes on Wednesdays. We played tennis every Saturday. She bought a Mercedes, I bought a BMW. We were young, wealthy, and had the world by the short and curlies.

Inevitably, after about a year, once our home was finally complete, Ava was bored. I gradually found our conversations veering more and more often toward the ancient art of baby makin'. Truth is, despite the exaggerated dread I affected every time the subject came up (just to bust Ava's cute little chops), the baby talk didn't bother me. We were both really excited about the idea. I'd always said I wouldn't even consider it until we could afford it, and now we could afford it. Heck, we could afford fifty of 'em.

Baby making, as it turned out, was a lot of fun. Once we decided to go for it, we really went for it with gusto. We did it in the morning, we did it in the evening. Sometimes I'd pop home for a quick one during lunch. Some people say that they get tired of all the sex in the pursuit of a baby. Those people are nuts. I felt like a lottery winner. Sure, I couldn't wait for a baby, but for the time being, I was enjoying all the makin'.

"Honey, we need to talk," Ava told me somberly one night as I walked through the front door after work, about two months after we decided to start trying. The look on her face felt like a punch in the gut, but in my typical way, I tried to keep it light.

"You're finally leaving me for Dicky?" We had a running joke that she was desperately in love with Dicky when in reality she had an intense dislike for him. She found his spoiled, loud, womanizing ways highly offensive and utterly unattractive.

"Yes. And also, I'm going to take a large fork and stick it into my eyeball and then pluck it out and eat it."

"Ouch."

"Yah. No. Honey, this is serious." My stomach dropped. The look on her face wasn't a joke.

"Is everything okay?"

She looked down at the floor, seeming to be working up the courage to tell me something terrible. Her chest heaved with the weight of what she was about to tell me. I went to her and grabbed her hands, which hung at her sides. She didn't look up. I swallowed hard, and prepared myself.

"Ava?" I finally asked.

She looked up at me . . . and smiled. And I knew.

I think Ava changed at that very moment. It was like the smile that stretched across her face lit a candle within her that glowed for the next nine months straight.

"We did it?"

"We did it! I'm pregnant! *We're* pregnant!" she said, and I picked her up and spun her around right there in the foyer.

We stopped spinning, and I looked her in the eyes. "Is it Dicky's?"

"No, honey," she said. "You made this one all by yourself."

"Dammit. It coulda been such a handsome kid."

She grabbed my face and got serious. "This is gonna be the most beautiful, luckiest kid in the whole world."

"That's the truth. You're gonna be the best mommy Beverly Hills has ever seen."

We kissed. And then I held her as tightly as I could, my eyes closed, savoring the moment.

"Is it real, Bobby? Is this really happening?" she whispered to the side of my head.

"Yes, baby. It's real. It's reeeeeally happening."

"We are so lucky."

And she was right.

At least for a while.

CHAPTER
Four

Jack Benjamin Flopkowski entered the world on August 30th, 2000, weighing in at seven pounds, two ounces. I remember the first time I saw him, thinking that his tiny fingers looked like mealworms. In retrospect, that doesn't sound all that adorable, but *man,* it sure seemed precious at the time.

Granted, I was a pediatrician, and had seen literally hundreds of newborn babies, and I should have been desensitized to the whole process. But despite all of my experience in the baby department, out popped this kid and the tears just started flowing from my eyes like someone had taken the cap off of a fire hydrant in my skull. He was beautiful. Right out of the womb he had a full head of beautiful flaxen hair. I always found that all newborn babies look like Winston Churchill, but not our Jack. He was perfect. Like a mini–George Clooney. It was clear from the start that he'd gotten his mama's genes, lucky fella.

We took him home a couple of days after he was born and those were bar none the best days of my life. I couldn't work the long hours I'd worked in the past knowing what was waiting for me at home. He was an easy, cheerful baby from the get-go. I've never seen smiles and laughter from a child so young. He made my heart swell with a love and pride like I'd never known before. I was darting home from the office in between patients just to hold my baby boy for a few minutes. Just to look at his smiling face and kiss his rosy cheeks and smell his fuzzy hair. I would always sing the song "You Are So Beautiful" to him. That was our song. Ava made fun of me whenever I did it (my voice sucks), but I could tell that Jack loved it. He always smiled when I sang it to him. So I sang it to him every day.

We spoiled the heck outta that little guy. There were more toys and clothes and baby gadgets in that house by the time he got home from the hospital than I had my entire childhood.

I grew up in a pretty poor, rundown part of Brooklyn. My dad was a plumber and my mother a secretary at the local high school. They were blue-collar folks who worked their tails off all day and came home and made sure we all three sat and ate dinner together each and every night. My dad grew up poor in a shack in the middle of nowhere, Oklahoma. A cowboy gone to live in the city. He carried a flask of whisky and chewed tobacco and collected guns. We had a cow skull hanging over our fireplace. He met my mom when he was on leave from the navy, while at port in New York, and once his tour was done, they got married and that's where he stayed. My father wasn't your typical corn-shuckin' hick. He was a very bright and deep-thinking fellow. He was also a little bit . . . eccentric. He always seemed to be deeply involved in whatever was going on in his own mind. He didn't talk much. He paced and mumbled and scribbled a lot of little notes to himself in a notebook he always carried in his pocket. If you didn't know him you might think he was a tad crazy. We'd eventually come to find out that he was. Dad had a quirky and—for lack of a better word—a *gruff* vibe about him. He wasn't a *mean* guy, never hit me or anything, he was just . . . tired. Tired and poor and angry at the world. He worked his ass off to keep us warm and well fed, and he felt that those were the sum of his duties to fulfill his role as father and husband.

Dad never intended to be a plumber and a tenement-dwelling family man. He was a writer at heart. He had big dreams. He'd been working on a novel for over twenty years called *The Human Being*. It was his passion. His dream. His ticket to a better life. He never showed us a single page of his writing, but I think it was the only thing he ever truly cared about. He told me once in a drunken haze that "A legacy is the only thing that matters in this world, son. It don't matter how many kids you have—they'll die at some point. Don't matter how many toilets you fix or how many broads you notch on your belt or how much loot you got under your mattress. It's all temporary. Only thing that matters is what you leave behind for the world. Your mark.

Otherwise you ain't worth shit and neither is the time you spent here."

The great tragedy was that my dad couldn't finish his beloved novel, and it eventually drove him crazy. Not just a little bit wacky like he'd been before. Clinically crazy. Slowly, painfully, catastrophically crazy.

He suffered in silence. He never showed me or Mom the extent of how tortured he truly was. Frustrated, yes. Odd, definitely. There was the pacing and the note scribbling. The sleepless nights. There were mood swings and bursts of anger. But we never knew how hopeless he'd become.

Sometimes, near the end of his life, he'd disappear for days at a time and my mom would tell me that he was out doing research for his book, but when he came back he always looked more drained and exasperated than he had before. He'd come home from work, eat dinner with us, and retire to the little "office" he'd built out of the closet in their bedroom. I remember the muffled sound of the typewriter keys coming through my thin bedroom wall, the sound that I fell asleep to every single night of my life. His only real goal was to finish that damned book he was writing.

But he just couldn't do it.

When I was fifteen my father killed himself in that little office by putting one of his beloved guns to his temple and pulling the trigger. He had a dark sense of humor, I guess, because in his will he left me the only copy of his manuscript and one of his guns. Like a challenge for me to finish that asinine fucking novel, and if I couldn't, there was always the gun . . .

I wasn't interested in following my father's troubled footsteps. I locked that manuscript away and never even cracked it open.

And my mom, she was never the same after my dad died. She passed away three years later from a broken heart. I believe that she waited just long enough for me to be considered an adult before she threw in the towel.

While Ava was pregnant I would often lie awake and worry that I would lapse into a similar pattern of disinterest with my child. I'd work all day and come home exhausted, too wiped to help my kid with his homework or toss the ball around in the yard. Let me tell you, the instant I saw that little face for the first time all of my worries and insecurities about fatherhood vanished. I knew I would love and cherish and nurture and spoil my child every day of his life. I was going to drink out of a mug that said WORLD'S BEST DAD and know that I'd earned it.

I didn't mind changing his diapers, or waking up in the middle of the night to feed him or rock him back to sleep. In fact, I remember feeling like there wasn't enough I could do to even *begin* to compare with the work that Ava was putting in. And Ava. Oh, Ava. Let me tell you about Ava! This was one hot mama. Motherhood really suited her. We didn't have a ton of sex during her pregnancy, but afterward, woo boy! I couldn't keep my hands off her! I couldn't put my finger exactly on what it was that had changed, but in that first year after Jack was born, Ava became a woman. In nine months she'd evolved from looking like an attractive co-ed to an absolute MILF.

And again, I know this all seems a bit too shiny and joyous. Was life really that good? I had a gorgeous, healthy child; a beautiful, adoring wife; a big, luxurious house; and a successful, flourishing medical practice. Yes, life really was that good.

That is, of course, until it was really bad.

CHAPTER
Five

I just can't get over how much this looks like Jack!" Ava said. It was a week before my fortieth birthday, and Ava was throwing a party for me at our house on the big day. We were looking at an enormous blown-up photo of me as a baby, sitting in a bathtub, mugging for the camera. Ava found the picture in an old album and had it enlarged and put on a five-foot by four-foot foam core board so all of our friends could sign it at the party. Jack was now roughly the same age as I was in the picture, and the resemblance was striking.

"You kiddin' me? *Much* uglier than Jack," Dicky added from behind us. He was sitting on a stool at the breakfast bar in our kitchen, wearing a black turtleneck sweater and drinking a glass of red wine. He was also wearing what I can only describe as a hideously ugly fishing hat. It had a camouflage pattern and a wide floppy brim and a band around the dome that looked like it could be used for holding hooks or bait. It did not look good on him.

"No kidding," I added. "The resemblance doesn't bode well for the Jackster."

"Oh please," Ava added, wrapping her arms around me and grabbing my butt with both hands. "He'll be lucky to be *half* as handsome as his daddy-o." She kissed me and gave my butt a squeeze.

"Enough, you two sweeties, you're making my teeth hurt," Dicky said with a fake smile.

"Oh zip it, Dicky," said Ava. "Your bad vibes will wake the baby." Jack was sound asleep in a bassinet in the part of our kitchen that Ava referred to as "the hang-out area." It contained a couch and a love seat and a lacy-bottomed ottoman. I spent many hours sitting on that couch with my legs up on the ottoman, staring at my boy sleeping peacefully in my arms. It seemed we were especially blessed in that regard. The kid could pass out like a champ.

"Please, honey, an earthquake epicentered in Beverly Hills couldn't wake that kid," said Dicky with a smirk.

"Why is he here?" asked Ava, jerking a thumb at Dicky, and only half joking.

"I think a more important question is: why is he wearing that stupid-lookin' hat?" I added with a laugh.

"I'm here, in this stupid hat, my darlings, to give our man Dr. Floppy here his fortieth b-day gift."

"Awww, that's so nice! Honey, he dressed like an idiot for you for your birthday!" Ava cracked. "Can I take a picture so we can enjoy it always?" We laughed and I gave her a playful tickle-squeeze.

"Quiet, woman. You wouldn't know anything about this sort of gift. It's manly stuff. You stay here in the kitchen where you belong, while Floppy and I go out back and be macho."

"Please allow the door to hit you in the ass on the way out, macho man," she said, as Dicky escorted me through the kitchen toward the door that led to the backyard.

"I think she likes me," he said as he closed the back door behind us.

"You think?"

"If she wasn't your wife I'd hate-fuck the shit outta her."

"Whoaaaa, buddy!"

"Sorry, Flop, it's true. Usually when a woman gives me as much shit as she does, we end up in the backseat of my car."

"Your Porsche? A little small, no? Wait, are you implying—"

"Yes. There's a good chance that your wife wants to fuck me."

We walked on the deck that was attached to my house and I followed him over to the side and down a set of stairs onto the grass. My backyard was large, surrounded by a copse of trees.

"Really? Because I sort of think she would rather stab you."

"Same difference, homeslice. That sort of ignorance is why you are tied to a ball and chain and I go home with a different woman every night."

"Well, ignorance is bliss, then, I suppose."

"No, pal. Fucking two twenty-year-old blondes with fake double-Ds at once while their fat friend cooks you dinner is bliss. Close your eyes." I shut my eyes and he came up behind me, put his hands on my shoulders, and guided me a few more steps.

"Okay. Open up!"

Sprawled on the lawn before me was a very large yellow camping tent.

"Voilà!" said Dicky.

"We having a slumber party in my backyard?" I asked.

"Nah, pal! We're goin' on a trip. A big one."

I looked at him curiously with a smile forming on my lips. "Where we going?"

"Come on in and I'll tell you!" He unzipped the flap of the tent and crawled inside. I followed. It was quite roomy in there. There were two sleeping bags laid out on the floor. "Okay, Flop. Check it out. Top-o'-the-line everything. North Face Expedition 36 tent. Super-light-weight four-man, four-season tent tested to negative sixty degrees Fahrenheit. *Plus,* two Valandre Freja sleeping bags *with hoods.* The lightest bags in the expedition series, windproof, waterproof, insulated with 850-fill-power goose down for a superior warmth-to-weight ratio, tested to negative twenty-two degrees Fahrenheit." He flopped onto his back on one of the bags. "Huh? Whaddaya think?"

"What do I think? I think it's awesome! Where the heck we going? Patagonia?"

"Nah, pal. Big Bear."

"California?" I asked. "Why not just go right out there?" I pointed to the patch of woods behind my house.

"Ahh, c'mon! I'm takin' you camping!"

"This is overkill, no? We could hike Everest with this gear!"

"Only the best for my boy! We're going camping for three nights. Gotta do it right! You're lucky—almost bought you a twenty-five-foot Airstream!"

"Oh, jeez."

"The tent and the bag are yours to keep. I bought a whole fuckload of fishing gear and assorted camping paraphernalia, too. You and me? We're gonna go out there and fuck Mother Nature in the ass!"

"Sounds . . . sounds like fun. I think. When we going?"

"Three weeks. I already got preapproval from your boss in there for the weekend of the 19th."

"I want to give you a thank-you hug but I think it might be awkward while lying here in this tent."

"Yeah. I'll pass on the tent-hug. Thank-you noted. It's gonna be great."

I bet he was right. It would've been great.

After Dicky left, Ava ran out to the market and I decided to check my email. Dicky and I had recently set up a website for our practice, and we were finding that while it was good for business, putting our email addresses on the site also gave our patients yet another way to bother us at home.

I was plodding through a long list of new messages when I came across a familiar name. It was from someone named Katie Turner, and the subject was "Hello Stranger."

Katie Turner, I thought. Could it be? I opened the email.

> Dear Dr. Robert Flopkowski (DR!?!?!?),
> How the hell r ya? This is a voice from your past. Remember me? I'm the freckle-faced girl who taught you how to kiss. Ring any bells? Man I hope this is the same Bobby Flopkowski.
> XO,
> Katie Turner

I couldn't contain the shit-eating grin that had snuck up and planted itself on my face. Katie Turner lived in the apartment across the hall from my family throughout my childhood. She was my first crush. My first kiss. My first girlfriend. Certainly the first girl I ever loved. I hadn't seen/heard/probably-even-thought-about Katie Turner in over twenty years. And now here she was! Through the magic of the Internet. *Y2K curse, my ass.*

I considered how to respond. I glanced at her email again and realized that it had arrived in my in-box less than five minutes ago.

I hit "Reply" and typed:

> Wait a minute . . . WHO taught WHO how to kiss?

I considered what else to write, and then decided

I liked the playfulness of the response as it was, and I clicked "Send."

I moved on to the next several emails in my in-box, mostly junk mail and emails from patients. When I heard the telltale "You've got mail!" I went back to the in-box.

Katie Turner. Re: Hello Stranger.

I opened it.

OMG! That was fast! I can't believe I actually tracked you down! Looks like you live in Los Angeles now. True? Are you on instant messenger? My screen name is katieturn321.

I opened up Instant Messenger. Clicked on "Add Buddy." Typed in her screen name and hit ENTER. And there she was. I thought about what to type.

DrBobby2424: must be a different dr. bobby. I live in Texas.

It took about ten seconds and then my computer made a *bing-bong-bing* sound and up popped:

Katieturn321: nuh uh shut up!
DrBobby2424: kidding. California dreamin.
Katieturn321: BOBBO!!!!!!!!!!!!!!
DrBobby2424: hiya!
Katieturn321: I CANT blieve I am talking to u rt now! OMG!

DrBobby2424: the internet rules
Katieturn321: omg I love it!!!!
DrBobby2424: so? How are you?
Katieturn321: well............ I guess I'm ok!
DrBobby2424: just ok?
Katieturn321: just moved to LALA land

I must admit now, in retrospect, I'm not sure why, but my heart sort of skipped a beat when I read that.

DrBobby2424: get outta here!
Katieturn321: c'mon Bobbo, I just got here!
DrBobby2424: lol. What r u doing here?
Katieturn321: well............ long story............
DrBobby2424: try me

She didn't respond for about ten seconds. I got the hint.

DrBobby2424: ok ok
Katieturn321: too long for IM. Maybe over coffee?

Before I considered how Ava might feel about that, I typed:

DrBobby2424: ABSOLUTELY!
Katieturn321: omg so exciting!
DrBobby2424: where do you live?
Katieturn321: well............nowhere yet......... Just moved here. staying in a motel in Hollywood for now

DrBobby2424: k. have a car?
Katieturn321: nope

Ugh. Being car-less in Los Angeles is like being leg-less in a figure-skating competition. Looked like I would be driving east.

DrBobby2424: how u getting around?
Katieturn321: friend or taxi.
DrBobby2424: ok. how bout we meet for lunch tomorrow? Could u get to a restaurant in, say, Beverly Hills?
Katieturn321: ooooooh fancy! Yeah. should be no prob.
DrBobby2424: great! Meet me at mr chow on Camden and Wilshire, tomorrow at 1?
Katieturn321: yayyy! Perfecto!
DrBobby2424: looking forward to seeing u Katie
Katieturn321: you too DOCTOR Bobbo!
DrBobby2424: ciao
Katieturn321: bye! xoxoxoxoxoxo

I logged off with a funny feeling in the pit of my stomach. Katie Turner! My first everything. In Los Angeles.

This would be interesting.

CHAPTER
Six

My first mistake: I didn't tell Ava. I don't know why. I just didn't. It was a completely harmless lunch with an old friend, and I knew that Ava would get bent out of shape about it because Katie was my ex-girlfriend and Ava knew her name from old stories and I just figured it was best left unsaid. Why stress her out about something so innocuous. Right?

As I drove to Beverly Hills the next day, that nervous feeling returned. I wondered what she was going to look like now. She was such a beautiful kid. Freckle-faced, reddish brown wavy hair, always in pigtails. She wasn't girly, but not a tomboy, either. She had a way of carrying herself that was just so damned cute. The girl had cute shooting out of her freakin' ears. I was so head over heels in love with her when I was a kid it was silly. I wasn't the best-looking guy in the building, nor the best athlete, nor the most popular, but luckily for me Katie always loved me back. I think she was the sole reason I was even semipopular. Being with her always gave me some instant cachet. People thought I was cooler than I actually was. Heck, *I* thought I was cooler than I actually was. She and I would walk hand in hand down our street and I would imagine people were staring at me, jealous. We would kiss in the stairwells. We would lie on the tar roof and look at the lack of stars. Katie and I used to sneak across the hallway to one or the other's apartment at night and make out for hours. We were together right up until the ninth grade, when her family moved to Long Island. I never saw her again. Until now.

I pulled up to Mr Chow in my big BMW a few minutes before one p.m., and there she was. I'm not sure why, but I pretended like I didn't see her, although everyone for a block in each direction could probably see that beaming grin she had going on. As I walked past, trying to play it cool, stomach churning, she said, "Bobby?"

I turned to her and smiled. My heart was hammering.

"Katie Turner. Wow."

"Bobby Flopkowski, MD," she said, and we hugged.

Truth is, up close, she didn't look so great. I mean, yeah, there was still some beauty there somewhere, but it seemed to be buried. She looked . . . I don't know, *tired*. Not just that, though. It's hard to put into words what I mean exactly, but she looked sort of *dulled*. Like a chalk drawing that had been wiped off a chalkboard but not fully erased.

She had dark circles under her eyes, and she was

too thin. The freckles were still there, though. Man, I used to love those freckles. Her lips were fuller than I remembered, but sort of puffy and chapped. Her eyes were green and her hair was wavy and the color of caramel. Her clothes were mostly black and kind of loose and ill fitting. She sort of looked like a mouse. A mouse that had the potential to be very cute, but had been through the wringer. No, she wasn't the same little innocent girl I once knew. I could tell she was examining me, too, and I momentarily wondered if I was getting a better internal review from her than she was getting from me.

"You look amazing," she said.

That settled that.

"Thank you, Katie! You do, too!"

Liar.

"Oh, shut up, liar." (That settled that.) "I'm well aware of how I look."

"Wh-what?" I stammered, feeling like she'd read my mind.

"I'll tell you all about it over lunch."

My mind flashed to our IM conversation the night before. I asked her why she'd moved here. *Long story,* she'd said. *Too long for IM.*

I was saved by a potentially awkward moment when the maître d' said, "Welcome back to Mr Chow, Dr. Flopkowski." I was a regular in those days. Katie raised an impressed eyebrow.

"Thanks, Peter," I said to the maître d'. He nodded politely and told us to follow him. I noticed that he gave her outfit a quick Beverly Hills look up and down as he rounded his little pulpit, and I felt embarrassed for her, because she saw it, too. She folded her arms over her chest and meekly followed Peter to our table.

"I don't quite fit in here, I guess," she said quietly once we were seated with black napkins unfolded in our laps by the extremely attentive waitstaff.

"Oh, stop, you're fine! What are you talkin' about?"

"'Welcome back, Dr. Flopkowski,'" she mocked, looking all stiff and obnoxious like the pretentious maître d'.

"Oh, stop," I said. I was suddenly feeling a sort of shame for pulling up in my big, expensive car with my thousand-dollar suit and gold watch, while she was looking so . . . well, *poor.*

"No, it's okay, Bobby. You don't have to be protective of me. I'm a tough chick."

"I know you are. I remember that time in—what was it, like, seventh grade?—you kicked Mikey Davis in the balls for trying to touch your boobs."

"Ha! Yeah! I remember that! I didn't even have any boobs!"

"Trust me, I know." I winked at her. She laughed and smacked my arm and the tension was broken. For the moment, anyway.

She stopped laughing and took a deep breath. "The good old days," she said sadly, looking down into her water glass and drawing circles on its damp side with the tip of her pointer finger.

"So. Tell me. What brings Katie Turner back into my life after all these years?" I asked.

"Well, long story," she said. There it was again. *Long story.*

"Okay. Do you want to talk about it?"

"Later. You first. Tell me everything. How did my first boyfriend from our shitty little tenement in Brooklyn become the Doctor King of Beverly Hills?"

"Oh, hardly!"

"'Welcome back, Dr. Flopkowski,'" she mocked again, a glimpse of her old confidence returning. "'Oh, thank you, *Peter.*'"

I laughed and thought about it for a moment and then said, "Well, I guess you could say I owe it all to you."

She arched an eyebrow and said, "Oh, I like it! Do tell!"

"Well, when you moved away, I lost the one thing that made me 'cool.' Without the hot girlfriend I was just some dorky little freshman in high school with not too many friends and not too much confidence. Since I wasn't running with the cool kids, it sort of forced me to hit the books."

"Ahh. So you're saying I turned you into a social outcast."

"Precisely. Which, in turn, made me study more. Which led to college, which led to becoming a doctor."

"Seems like I should get a cut of your salary."

"I'll check with my boss about that."

"Your boss? Based on that nifty little website of yours I thought you *were* the boss. You and your partner, right? What, does he wear the pants or something?"

"No, no. I was referring to my wife. 'Honey, I've decided to give a cut of my salary to my ex-girlfriend.' Yeah . . . don't think that would go over well."

"Your wife, huh?" Maybe I was imagining it, but I could have sworn I saw her sink a little bit in her seat. Like I'd just dashed some secret hope.

"Yep. Seven years. Ava. We just had a baby, too. His name's Jack. He's eleven months."

"Oh my God! Wow, Doc. Sounds like you've carved out quite the little life for yourself out here in sunny California."

"Yeah, I guess I have," I tried to say in a way that would sound more proud than conceited.

"Well, I think that's great," she said. "I can't wait to meet your baby." We looked each other in the eyes and I could see that although she was genuinely happy for me, there was immense pain there, too.

We were interrupted by the waiter, who brought us our first course. You don't order at Mr Chow, they just keep bringing you stuff until you say uncle. The first course was minced chicken in lettuce cups with this delicious sweet plum sauce. We devoured it. We bullshitted our way through the next few mini-courses, laughing about kids from our old building and all the weirdo grown-ups and assorted wack jobs that our neighborhood seemed to produce, and then about halfway through some sort of delightful shrimp dish, mouth full, she was finally ready to spill the beans.

"So you ready for my tale of woe?"

"You know, Katie, you don't have to tell me anything you don't want to tell me. I completely understand if you don't want to talk about it."

"No, it's okay."

"Good, because I really want to know."

She laughed and then said, "Well, lonnnnnng story short"—she took a deep breath here, then continued—"I fell on some real hard times, Bobbo." *Bobbo*. That's what she'd always called me growing up. We'd slipped back into an old pattern of comfort, which was surprising being that we hadn't seen each other in over twenty years.

"Hard times, how?"

"Well, things changed after we moved. I did a lot of drugs in high school. Started out innocently enough, you know, the basics: drinkin', smokin', tokin', you've heard all this before."

"Right . . . ?"

"And then my dad died when I was in twelfth grade, and I did a fucking tailspin. I got into heavier drugs, I started sleeping around. You know, typical teenage angsty rebel bullshit, but kinda worse." She looked sad now, and the rings under her eyes seemed to have gotten darker. I thought about my own father, and realized that Katie was already gone when he committed suicide. I wondered if she even knew about it. "I got involved with sort of a sleazy group. I graduated high school by the skin of my teeth and went to Nassau Community College out on the island. Lived in an apartment with two other dirtbaggy chicks and for a few years straight did every drug under the sun. Speed, acid, coke, shrooms, pot, pain killers, Ecstasy—*lots* of Ecstasy—Special K, meth . . . *everything*. Every thing, every day."

"Jeez."

"You ain't heard nothin' yet, Bobbo."

My eyebrows rose. I couldn't believe the wildly different paths Katie and I had taken. The deaths of our fathers sent us in opposite directions. I took control and vowed to myself that I wouldn't end up like my father, while she'd completely lost control. Visions flashed in my mind of her all messed up on drugs and getting fucked by disgusting drug dealers.

"So obviously, it's no surprise that I ended up dropping out of school. Then I started working nights at a strip club." She saw me pale, and said, "Not as a *stripper*, Bobbo. As a waitress."

"Nah, that's cool, whatever. Doesn't matter to me. I don't judge."

But it *did* matter. I was relieved.

"Anyway, I was still all fucked up on drugs, and lo and behold, I got pregnant. Shocker! I know. I didn't even remember who I'd had sex with. No clue. Anyway, I was already close to six months pregnant by the time I found out." The doctor alarm in my head was going ballistic. *Six months pregnant before she found out? How fucked up on drugs do you have to be to not know you're pregnant for six months? And what effect did that have on the baby?*

"Did you quit the drugs?"

"Yes. Of course! Went stone-cold sober the day I found out. Moved home with my mom. Took care of myself like I'd never done before for the next three months."

"Good. I'm so glad to hear that."

"No. It was too little too late. My baby was stillborn." She said it without emotion.

I reached across the table and grabbed her hand. "Oh my God. Katie, I am so sorry."

She swallowed hard and inhaled deeply through her nose, but she didn't shed any tears. I got the feeling that Katie had already done all the crying she would ever do over this.

"It was rough. Terrible. I'd already had a name picked out and everything. His name was Steven. After my father."

As a pediatrician, I had seen this happen before, but only twice. There is *nothing* more tragic and heart shattering than seeing a dead infant. Nothing.

"So yeah. I didn't take it well. I went right back to the drugs with a vengeance. Took it to a whole new level. Started doing heavier shit. Morphine, Demerol, Oxy-Contin . . ." She scratched her head like she could recall the feeling of being on all those drugs. "I mean, I was taking more drugs than a cancer patient to kill my pain. But it wouldn't go away. And so . . . like a stereotypical little depressed drug addict, I moved on to the big one: heroin."

All I could do was nod my head. I had a feeling that was where this was going.

"I did a lot of bad things after that, Bobbo. For a lot of years. Things I don't remember and things I don't want to remember. I hurt myself and I hurt everyone who loved me."

"But you lived. Most people don't."

"I know. Ain't that just the craziest part? Cuz I didn't want to, Bobbo. I didn't want to and I didn't *intend* to."

"How'd you stop?"

"It's more *why* I stopped."

"Okay, *why'd* you stop?"

"I stopped because I had an epiphany."

"Which was?"

"I had to have a child to replace the one I lost."

I raised my eyebrows and nodded.

"I know this is going to sound like crazy talk from a drug addict, but I had a vision. Yeah, I was all fucked up at the time, but still. I had a vision of my future child. I saw him, and it was real, and I knew what I had to do."

"When was this?"

"About a year ago."

"So what did you do?"

"I went to my mom's, where I hadn't been in almost three years. And after she finished crying her eyes out, she checked me into rehab."

"So you're completely clean now?"

"Been clean for ten months."

"So why are you here? In Los Angeles, I mean?"

"I'm here to start over, Bobbo. Clean slate, new place. And I'm here because of a guy." She flashed that one-thousand-watt smile again.

I smiled, too. "Tell me!"

"His name's Vincent. We met in rehab. Which I know sounds like a terrible idea, but he's amazing. And he's a guitar player and he's so talented and we moved here so he could give a shot at the big time."

I guessed I was wrong earlier when I was thinking that she wanted me. "Wow, Katie. That is really great. I'm really thrilled for you."

"Yeah, you know, it's cool. This is the best I've felt in years. Probably since you knew me. We'll see where it goes. First I'd like to find a place to live. Vincent is crashing with an old buddy of his, but it's a studio apartment, so . . . you know." She rolled her eyes. "Three's a crowd." The notion briefly crossed my mind that I could offer her the use of one of the many spare bedrooms in our house, but there was no way I could do that without asking Ava.

We finished our meal, I paid the tab, and as we walked outside discussing how we most certainly had to get together again soon, it dawned on me that I could invite her to my birthday party the following week, and so I did. She was thrilled. We hugged good-bye.

"Hey!" someone yelled from a dingy car that had pulled up to the curb in front of the restaurant. We both turned to look. The car was old, rusty, and loud as hell. I had to bend down a bit to see the driver. He wore large black sunglasses, had long, greasy black hair, a goatee, and several piercings in both ears. He was wearing a black tank top, and his arms were covered with tattoos. He squinted to avoid the smoke curling up from the burning cigarette in his lips.

I didn't think he was talking to us, until:

"Vincent!" Katie shouted gleefully. She bolted over to the car, and pulled me by the hand. We ducked down so we were both peeking through the passenger-side window.

"Bobby, this is my boyfriend, Vincent! Vincent, this is the famous Dr. Bobby I've been telling you about!"

I reached my hand in to shake Vincent's. He looked at my hand, almost in disgust, and finally shook it, dead-fish style.

"It's really nice to meet you, Vincent. Katie told me all about you."

"Yeah?" he asked.

"Yeah," I said, in my most cheerful voice. I have to admit, this guy scared me. He gave off a vibe of violence and general repugnance.

"You enjoy that nice long hug?" he asked, with a jerk of his head toward the sidewalk where Katie and I had been standing.

"Vincent! Stop it!" Katie said, smacking him playfully in a way that indicated she thought he was joking.

Vincent glared at me. He wasn't joking.

"Well, I gotta run. Nice to meet you, Vincent," I said without looking at him. He didn't return the sentiment.

Katie gave me another hug, which I returned awkwardly, bracing for the stabbing that was surely coming my way from Vincent.

"I'll see you at your party!" said Katie as she got in his car.

I got in my own car and drove away, feeling like I'd just been through the wringer myself.

CHAPTER

Seven

Ava did a terrific job setting up the house for the party. She hired a lighting company to string little balls of light all around our backyard. She hired a catering company to set up an incredible buffet full of gourmet food, and about eight waiters to bring around all sorts of tasty appetizer morsels on trays. There were two separate, fully stocked bars. There was an ice sculpture in the shape of a giant "4" and a giant "o" sitting atop an elaborately carved base. And to top it off, there was a dance floor and a five-piece band belting out tunes. I'm not much of a party animal, but this was one classy soiree, if I do say so myself.

We hired a sitter for the night to watch Jack. He was asleep before the party even started and slept right through the night. The sitter, a woman named Bree, had nothing to do but read gossip magazines all evening.

Maybe it was a waste of a hundred bucks, but we were happy to not have to worry about the baby during the party.

Everyone we knew was there. I spent the first hour or two doing the social-butterfly thing, flitting around from group to group, shaking hands, hugging, taking all the ribbing about my new elderly status. Dicky and I kept sneaking off to my office where we could swig off of an absurdly expensive bottle of scotch that he'd brought. Like I said, I wasn't much of a party animal, and that included the socializing part of the equation. The whisky made it easier.

I should have eaten more of the appetizers, because before I knew it, I was drunk. I could tell that people were getting a kick out of it. Doctors spend most of the time being serious, so I guess people were enjoying the looser version of Dr. Bobby. After my third or fourth trip to the office with Dicky, I was having a damned fine time.

Ava and I did some dancing, she read a very sweet speech she'd written for me, and then we did some more dancing.

"You're hammered!" she giggled in my ear, enjoying my saucy party mode.

"Nooooooo!" I said, as the singer crooned a remarkably good version of "I Heard It Through the Grapevine," sounding so much like Fogerty that if I weren't looking at the guy I might have believed that my wife had hired Creedence to play my party.

"Okay, yeah. I definitely am," I said, both of us laughing now.

"Let's go get you some water and something to put in your belly, birthday boy."

As she pulled me by my hand off of the dance floor, I spotted Katie walking out of the house into the backyard for the first time that night. *She's here!* I thought. She looked . . . well, maybe it was the alcohol, but she looked *beautiful.* Gone was the tired, beaten-down woman I'd had lunch with a week ago. She was wearing a form-fitting black party dress, and her hair was pulled back in a tight ponytail. She looked like she'd gotten a little suntan. *Boy, she cleans up well.* I was relieved she hadn't brought that creep Vincent with her. Ava spotted her, too, and whispered, "Who is *that?*" And it dawned on me that I hadn't even mentioned Katie to Ava yet. Nothing about the emails. Nothing about the IMs. Nothing about the lunch. I was suddenly feeling a tad nauseated.

"That's . . . that's Katie Turner!" I said, trying to act like we'd discussed it a thousand times.

"Who?" Ava asked.

"Katie Turner!" I said. "Remember? My old friend from Brooklyn! She's in town so I invited her!"

Ava's eyes narrowed ever so slightly and I could see that she now fully realized exactly who Katie was. Not just an old friend. She started to object, but Katie had spotted us and was making her way over.

"Wait a minute . . . Katie Turner, as in your first girlfr—"

"Katieeeeeeeeee! Heyyyy! You made it!" I slurred. I could feel Ava still looking at me, but then I saw her turn to Katie.

"Hey, Bobbo. Yep! I made it." She took a quick glance around the backyard and then said, "Long way from my crappy little motel on Hollywood Boulevard. And a *really* long way from Brooklyn!" Katie turned to Ava and extended her hand. "You must be Ava."

I looked at Ava, and though she was smiling in what looked like an authentic way, and I was drunk, I could still see that the wheels in her mind were spinning behind that smile.

"Yes! Hello, Katie! Welcome!" Ava said, and then turned to me as if to say, *Ummmm, why am I welcoming this gorgeous former girlfriend of yours to this party?*

"Thank you so much for having me," Katie said. "Bobby told me all about you over lunch the other day!"

BOOM. There it was. I felt Ava's hand tighten around mine, but I was too drunk to worry much about any of it.

"Ohh, that's nice!" Ava said. I have to give her credit—she was a good actress. "Please, come on in, help yourself to a drink and some food."

"No Vincent?" I asked, mostly just so Ava would know that she had a boyfriend.

"No, no. He had practice with his band."

"Oh, that's too bad," I said. *I'm sure it's a charming, whimsical little ensemble.*

"Make yourself at home," Ava said to Katie, before turning to me and sweetly adding, "*Bobbo,* would you come inside for a sec?"

"Go mungle!" I said to Katie, not having enough time to correct myself before being pulled away by my wife. Ava led me into my office, which was just a few doors down the hallway from the door to the yard, and closed the door behind us.

"Honey," she said in a saccharine way that to me indicated she might be a little bit peeved. I was sharp as a *tack*. "Care to tell me about lunch the other day with the incredibly attractive first love of your life?" She actually wasn't that mad. I mean, she was annoyed, but I think she was taking it easy on me because of the whole it's-a-big-party-in-my-honor thing. Still, this was definitely killing my buzz.

"Oh man, I am so sorry, honey. It wasn't intentional, I swear. I just forgot to tell you."

"How do you forget to tell me something like that, darling?"

"I don't know! It just, it wasn't a big deal. It was a quick, last-minute lunch in the middle of a hectic day, and I just forgot. I'm really sorry, hon."

She scrutinized my face. "It's your birthday, so you get a get-outta-jail-free card. But it woulda been nice to know that this gorgeous woman was going to show up here calling you 'Bobbo.'"

I pulled her in for a hug. "I'm sorry, honey. But listen—funny thing is—she *wasn't* gorgeous when I had lunch with her last week. She was a bit of a wreck, actually. She's been through hell the past few years. She's a recovering drug addict, and she just moved out here to start over and she doesn't really know anyone, and she's living in a motel and I just felt badly for her so I invited her. No biggie, right?"

She pulled out of our hug and looked me in the eyes and then grabbed my face with both hands and smiled. "No biggie, my cute little drunk birthday boy." She planted a kiss on my lips. "You're sweet. Let's go out there and party our butts off, old man."

"I'm way ahead of you," I said.

I tickled her and we giggled our way back to the yard. I didn't realize then that those were some of the last laughs we'd ever have together.

———————

Ava and I danced for what seemed like a very long time. Ava had specially requested "Gonna Make You Sweat (Everybody Dance Now)" by C+C Music Factory. We laughed and danced and I still looked like a total spaz after all these years. Before I knew it, I was sweating and exhausted. I saw that Katie was sitting at a table with Dicky, and I thought she looked uncomfortable, so I whispered to Ava, and we decided to go rescue her.

As I got closer and Katie spotted me, Dicky turned his head toward us, and behind his back Katie opened her eyes wide at us, confirming that she needed help.

"Hey! It's the crotchety old birthday boy!" Dicky said.

"That's me," I responded. "What are you young'uns doing over here? You look like you're up to no good."

"He's up to no good," Katie said. "I'm just trying to explain to him that I have a boyfriend."

"She has a boyfriend, Dicky," I said.

"Is there an echo out here?" Dicky sneered.

"Beat it, bud," I said. "I need to acquaint my first love to my last love." As I said it I knew it was the wrong thing to say. I shouldn't have been referring to Katie as my love in front of Ava. Stupid stupid stupid. I quickly threw an arm around Ava, who tensed.

"Fine, if I can't go home with the prettiest girl at the party, I'll just have to have a few more drinks until everyone is the prettiest girl at the party," said Dicky. Then he leaned over and whispered into my ear, "She may not want a cocktail, but she definitely wants a cock in her tail."

As I turned to give him a disapproving look he rose and said, "Ciao!" as he boogied back to the bar.

I turned to Katie. "I'm so sorry. I didn't think about all the drinking when I invited you. I didn't mean to—"

"Bobbo, please. Don't be silly. I can absolutely handle it," Katie said. "It's pretty funny to see you drunk, actually."

"Who knew he was such a lush!" said Ava, and they both laughed. I smiled but I didn't find it so funny. I was glad they were getting along, though, so I indulged them.

"Oh gee," I said in an exaggeratedly drunken way, moving my head in circles like I was even more wasted than I actually was. "I'm so glllad I'm so fffffffrrriggin' entertaining." I flopped down on the chair that Dicky had been sitting in, and they both laughed. Just then the photographer that Ava had hired snapped a picture of me looking like a drunken disaster, sprawled out on the little folding chair.

"Oh great!" I said, and the girls laughed even harder.

"That's a keeper!" said the gangly male photographer. I gave him a dirty look, and told him to scram.

Ava sat down next to me so we were sitting in a

triangle, and I said, "Anyway, we're so glad you came, Katie."

"Thank you guys again for having me," she replied. "Really, I don't think I've ever seen anything like this in my life!"

"All her," I said, gesturing to Ava with my thumb and then grasping her hand. "She's the mastermind."

"Oh, stop," Ava said. She was enjoying the attention I was lathering on her in front of Katie. We sat, the three of us, and talked for a while. Ava and I were both at that drunken point where we no longer felt like bouncing around the party. I was enjoying having the two great loves of my life in one place. It wasn't awkward at all, surprisingly. Quite the opposite, really. To my drunken mind, Ava and Katie seemed to be getting along splendidly. I watched them chitchatting without me and I smiled. An idea was bubbling in my alcohol-soaked brain. When I heard their conversation veer toward Katie's living accommodations, my ears perked up.

"So where are you staying?" Ava asked her.

"Oh, some motel on Hollywood Boulevard. It's called the Bed of Roses Inn," Katie said, looking embarrassed in front of her new friend, who obviously didn't stay at such places.

Ava is no snob, but in this situation, it's pretty difficult to not come off as one. "I've never heard of it," she said.

"Yeah, you wouldn't've," Katie replied. "It's, uh . . . it's . . . *yuck*," she said with a shiver. "It's all I can afford for now, though."

I looked at Ava, and I could've *sworn*. I repeat: I.

Could. Have. *Sworn* that she gave me the slightest little head nod. The go-ahead. We would debate this later. A lot. That split-second drunken decision was another tiny misstep that changed the course of the rest of my life.

"Katie, we have three extra bedrooms! Why don't you crash here for a bit, instead of that horrific motel, just until you find a place to live."

Ava's hand instantly tightened around mine, and I knew I'd fucked up. Badly.

CHAPTER
Eight

Of course, in the moment, Ava was forced to go along with it, and with our insistence, Katie cheerfully accepted our invitation. When the party was over and everyone was finally gone, I knew the fight was imminent. We were up in our bedroom, getting ready for bed, or at least I was. Ava was already in bed. I was drunk and struggling to get both legs into my boxer shorts when she launched the first volley.

"Honey?"

I was in the closet where Ava couldn't see me. I got my boxers on, stood up straight, and cringed. I *really* didn't want to get into it with her. "Yes, dear?" I said in a loaded way that I felt expressed that I knew what she was about to say and I didn't want to hear it.

"I think you know what I'm going to say," she said.

"Honey, I do know what you are going to say. I know

exactly what you are going to say"—I flopped down on the bed and flipped the covers up over me in one—okay, more like five—awkward movements—"and I am too drunk to have this conversation right now." The pillow felt like pure magic on my face. I knew I wasn't going to last long in the world of wakefulness. "Can we talk about it tomorrow?"

"Yes, but, *honey,* how could you ask a stranger to stay here without consulting . . ."

I didn't hear the rest of what she said, because I was asleep. Hello, bad move number three!

And what a pleasant morning it was.

Never mind the killer hangover, the likes of which I hadn't seen since college. It was Ava who really brought the pain. She was lying on her side in bed, staring at me when I woke up. Waiting. Like a cat. As soon as I opened my eyes and slowly turned my head toward her, she pounced.

"I need to know how a smart man such as yourself could possibly invite a *stranger*—a *drug addict*—into our home when we have an *infant* child!"

It took me a moment to remember what she was talking about. My next thought was, *Ava was pretty wasted last night, too! How could she be so ready to get into it right now?* And then I remembered: women have magical powers.

"Honey, listen."

"I am listening, *Bobbo,* and I want an answer. Your birthday is over and I want an answer. How?"

"How?" I asked. Not the best stalling tactic, but it was all I had.

"How?! How could you invite, not only a *drug addict*—"

"Recovering," I helpfully pointed out, as she rose from the bed.

"A *drug addict*," she repeated. "Who we *don't even know*, by the way, a *stranger*, into our *home*, where we live with our *infant fucking child*, Bobby—!"

She'd worked up some serious steam very quickly.

"And notice that I am leaving your secret lunch meeting out of this conversation. I'm forgiving you on that shady little encounter. But how did you end up reconnecting with this person, anyway?"

I exhaled deeply and considered my answer.

"Honey . . . I've known her since I was a little kid. She's not a stranger. She found me on the Internet. And she needs help."

"Oh, she found you on the Internet! Perfect! And that's just the kind of guy you are, huh? When a gorgeous damsel in distress who you haven't seen in—what, twenty-five years—tracks you down on the Internet, the brave and heroic Dr. Bobby is there to save the day!"

"Hon, that's not cool."

"What? Bobby, what's not *cool* is that you invited this woman to *live with us*! Without consulting me!"

"Hon—"

"No! That's the bottom line! I don't know this woman from a fucking hole in the wall! And last time I checked, this was a democracy!"

"Ava—"

"What? What could you possibly say here that will make this okay?"

I exhaled deeply again. She saw that as another

chance to attack. "Bobby, all the deep breaths in the world are not going to resolve the fact that I am not okay with this!"

"You know, I could have *sworn* that you gave me the go-ahead nod." Stupid stupid stupid.

"Excuse me? The 'go-ahead nod'? Are you out of your mind? I'm not your fucking third base coach, Bobby. Seriously, if you thought that, you should never drink again. Because it makes you into a psychotic idiot who imagines things that absolutely do not exist."

"Ava—"

"Really, Bobby? The 'go-ahead nod'? Are you serious? Is *that* your best argument?"

"Honey—"

"Pretty fucking weak."

I flopped my head back onto my pillow. I rubbed my forehead. I'd been awake for approximately forty-five seconds. I couldn't summon a logical argument. I took another deep breath and exhaled audibly.

Ava was ready for this response.

"Oh, that's right! You've got the exhale, also. Well, shoot, I'm convinced! When can the drug-addled supermodel move in, then? I don't know why I didn't see the genius and benevolence of this plan before!" She stomped over to the bedroom door. I thought she was simply going to exit and slam the door behind her. Instead, she turned around to issue this good-natured proclamation: "You know, for a doctor, you are one of the dumbest motherfuckers I have ever met in my entire fucking LIFE!"

And *then* came the slam.

CHAPTER
Nine

We didn't speak much in the days that followed our fight in the bedroom. Correction: Ava didn't speak much. She communicated mostly with grunts and nods and rolling eyeballs. I tried to work it out. I tried to apologize. I offered to rescind my invitation to Katie. I brought home flowers from work *every single day*. Flowers usually worked with Ava. But not this time. I'd burned a bridge in her brain and there was no turning back. I made my proverbial bed and now I would have to lie in it with my angry-ass wife sleeping next to me.

And then, five days after the party came move-in day, and things actually improved.

Katie knocked on our door around ten a.m. with a bag slung over her shoulder and a grin on her face. Ava answered the door and I followed her over there, anticipating the inevitable awkwardness. But then:

"Katie! Helloooo! Welcome!" said Ava.

I looked at her, surprised at this defrosted version of my wife.

"Hi, guys," said Katie. She looked nervous. But *hot,* too.

"We're *so* happy to have you here. Come on in, we'll show you to your room," Ava said, sweet and seemingly genuine as could be.

"Oh, Vincent is just getting my suitcase out of the car. He'll be right up."

Shit. I was pretty sure Vincent and Ava wouldn't be instant BFFs.

"Honey, why don't you show Katie the guestroom. I'll wait for Vincent," I said.

Ava and Katie departed for the guestroom, leaving me waiting for lovely Vincent. I knew this wasn't going to end well.

I smelled his cigarette before I saw him. Vincent swaggered right into my house with a lit ciggy stuck in his lips. "Where should I put this shit?"

"You can leave it there. And would you mind putting your cigarette out? We don't smoke in here."

Vincent rolled his eyes without actually rolling his eyes and flicked the cigarette right out the door into my shrubs. "Where's Katie?"

"Follow me," I said.

We walked to the guest bedroom, Vincent looking around and surely sizing up my house for robbery.

When we got to the room, the girls were chatting.

"Oh my gosh, *such* a different world from my motel!"

"I'm sure!" said Ava. "Well, please, get comfy and make yourself at home."

"Vincent, can you *believe* this?"

I walked over to Ava and she actually put her arm around my waist. I think it was the first time we'd touched since my birthday.

"Hi, Vincent, I'm Ava."

Vincent looked at Ava lecherously. I mean really *looked* at her. Up and down, like a piece of meat, the contempt and desire all over his dirty, oily face. He was practically licking his chops.

"Hey."

I thought, *Doesn't the whole angsty, emo thing usually end after high school? Kurt Cobain is dead, dude. Move on.*

"Vincent is in a grumpy mood today," said Katie. "He got in a fight with his drummer."

Vincent made a grumbling sound and said, "I gotta jet."

"Aww, too bad!" I said. Couldn't help it.

"We'll walk you out," said Ava. "Katie, you unpack."

Ava and I walked Vincent to the front door, both of us watching him with eyes peeled as he touched every surface, painting, statue, knickknack, and piece of furniture in his path.

"*So* nice to meet you, Vincent," said Ava, as we got to the door. Vincent just laughed. And then he left without another word.

"He's sweet." Ava didn't answer. "Honey, thank you for being so nice," I said, reaching for her hand. She snatched her arm away as soon as I touched her skin.

"Don't talk to me," she spat.

- - - - - -

And on it went like that for a couple of weeks. In front of Katie, Ava was a doll. But it was for Katie's benefit only. As soon as we were alone, I was persona non grata. In front of Katie, we were the freakin' Cleavers. No Katie, no speaky.

The problem was, Katie was a big reminiscer. Always talking about "Remember that time in eighth grade when we cut school and snuck into that hotel and found an empty room and made out for, like, five hours straight!? Oh my god, that was craaaazy! That was, like, the longest I've ever made out with anyone! Still! To this day!" I would smile and she would laugh and then I'd look at Ava fake-smiling and I could see the twin fires burning just behind her eyeballs. There were a few times when I thought laser beams might shoot out of her eyes or a lamp would just suddenly explode somewhere in the room.

Ava and I hadn't had a cordial conversation in about fifteen days. Every day she would play the good wife and I'd almost believe that things were going to be okay, but when we got into bed at night, I would lean in to kiss her good night, and she would turn over, pulling the blanket tightly around her like a force field that my very limited superpowers could not penetrate. I tried to initiate conversation, but it was like talking to a statue. A statue of a bitch. She made it very clear that until Katie was gone, our marriage was on hold.

Meanwhile, and I know this sounds like a terrible thing to say, but aside from my crumbling relationship with my wife, I was really enjoying having Katie around. Listen, to be clear, I loved my wife more than I've ever loved any woman in my life, and the silent treatment certainly sucked, but with Katie there, I couldn't help feeling like a kid with a crush again. And Katie felt it, too, I could tell. We were reconnecting. Rekindling an old flame. When Ava wasn't around shooting daggers at us, we would flirt and laugh and I could actually start to defrost from Ava's constant Ice Queen Routine.

One night after dinner, when Katie was out with Vincent, Ava was doing the dishes and I was clearing the table and I'd had a couple of beers with dinner and was feeling brave, so I said, "So is this how it's going to be from now on, huh, Ava?"

Her back to me, she shrugged her shoulders.

"Huh? Because I made one stupid, temporary mistake? This is now our life? This is the environment our child is going to be raised in?"

Ava said something under her breath to the tune of "It's not *my* fault our child is living in a house with strangers." It was the longest sentence she'd spoken to me in weeks.

"What? Did you say something?"

She scrubbed hard at a plate.

"Hon, I mean, come on! I *love* you. She'll be gone soon! I can't stand this!"

Ava spun around. "You know what I can't stand? I can't stand listening to you two lovebirds reminiscing about how fucking much you looooooved each other. How much you *learned* from each other. How you remember exactly how she used to *kiss*." I did an internal forehead slap when I recalled that I'd actually *said* something like that a few days prior. Stupid stupid stupid.

I stepped toward her and put a hand on one of her crossed arms. "Ava—"

"Don't," she said, and pulled away.

"Please, honey," I pleaded. "Tell me what to do and I'll do it."

"Bobby, you shoulda done it two weeks ago when I told you how I felt about this whole thing."

"I tried! You wouldn't *let* me!"

"You *tried?* How did you *try?*" she asked, her eyebrows raised.

"I told you I would rescind the invitation and you said not to!"

"Um, yeah, but do you think I would have been *more* or *less* upset than I am right now if you'd gone ahead and done it anyway?"

I thought about it, and she was undeniably correct, and I hated her twisted woman logic. But this was the first shot I'd had at redemption, and I wasn't going to blow it. I nodded my head. "You're right."

"Yeah, I know I'm right, Bobby. And my question is, *why* didn't you do it? Despite your recent behavior, you're not a stupid man. In fact, you're probably the smartest person I know. So what made you let this stranger—this drug addict—into our home? Are you unhappy in this marriage? Are you missing something? Did you hope to rekindle something with her? What? What is it? That's what I need to know, Bobby."

I rested one hand on the counter and looked down at my feet. I thought about how to answer that, but I couldn't think for too long because there was only one acceptable answer. "Of course I'm happy in our marriage, Ava. I love you. More than anything. I swear it was only a case of me trying to help out an old friend, and foolishly not thinking about how it would affect you. You know I don't think things through sometimes. And I'm honestly, truly sorry. I will tell her that she has to leave immediately."

"You are going on your camping trip in six days. She can stay until then. Give her that time to find somewhere else to go."

I stepped toward my wife, hoping I might just get a smile or a hug out of her. When I reached up for her she said, "No, Bobby. You don't get me back until she is gone and our lives can go back to normal again."

"Fair enough," I said with a polite, sad nod. "Fair enough." It was fun having Katie around and all, but I wanted my wife back.

— — — — — —

The next morning I asked Katie to lunch.

"Is this a date, Bobbo?" she asked flirtatiously. *I love my wife. I love my wife. I love my wife,* I thought. And I *did* love my wife. I can't emphasize that enough. It's just that . . . I don't know! I can't help but get a flutter in my belly when a beautiful woman flirts with me. Especially one that I still think about sometimes when I masturbate. Okay, I shouldn't have said that last part.

"I'm a married man, kiddo. In case you hadn't noticed."

"I've noticed, Bobbo. I'm just joshin'. Where to?"

We made a plan to meet at a place near my office. I got there early and sat at a small table outside. I was nervous. I mean, Ava was completely, 100 percent right. Katie needed to go. But I still couldn't help but feel *badly* about it. Like I was putting her back on the street. Katie arrived wearing a little clingy red dress thingy. It was tight around her chest and loose and flowing around her bottom half. Man, she looked great in everything. She touched my shoulder as she moved around the table, and gave me a surprise peck on the cheek. My hands were folded in front of me on the table, and when Katie was seated, she reached over and put one of her hands on top of mine. "Hey, Doc!" she said.

"Hey, cutie—uh, Katie," I said, blushing. Paging Dr. Freud. She was so much more suntanned than she'd been when I first saw her a few weeks prior. And her hair looked healthy and shiny. And her green eyes in contrast with her olive, freckled skin were just so . . . okay, I'll stop.

"Ohhhh, Bobbo. Stop it," she said, slapping my hands. She didn't realize that I hadn't meant to say "cutie." We both ordered iced teas, and I got right down to biz.

"Katie, you're probably wondering why I asked you to meet me."

"You're kickin' me out, huh?" She was smiling, and I was relieved.

I made an apologetic sort of face. "How'd you know?"

"Your wife isn't *that* good of an actress." I couldn't help but laugh. Here I'd thought we'd been fooling Katie the whole time with our *Leave It To Beaver* act. "And neither are you, Bobbo. Sorry." She was laughing, too, now.

And her hand was back on mine. And that's when Ava's best friend Christie happened to walk by.

Christie looked at me and did a double take and then she looked at Katie and her eyes went right down to our intertwined hands on the table. I snapped my hands back, startling Katie and Christie and looking totally busted.

"Christie! Hi!" I blurted.

"Helloooo, Robert . . ." She said this cautiously and awkwardly and without any attempt at hiding the fact that she didn't like what she was seeing. And when I say she didn't like what she was seeing I mean she actually *loved* what she was seeing. I didn't like what *I* was seeing because Christie is a gossipy, big-mouthed, shit-stirring bitch. With a puckered little half smile, Christie said, "And who is . . . ?"

I stood up for some reason and said, "Oh, Christie, this is Katie, my old friend who has been living, uh, staying with us for the past few weeks, and Katie, this is Christie Billingsgate, one of Ava's dear, dear friends."

Christie, ever the snob, reached out a drooping hand that looked like it should have been swathed in a long-sleeved glove toward Katie's extended, unmanicured hand, and, without looking at her, said, "Oh? Living with you? Ava never mentioned *that*." She dragged out the word "that" in such a way that implied this piece of information was gossip gold. And I knew that I'd somehow just managed to fuck this situation up a little bit more.

"Oh no?" I asked, hoping my voice wasn't cracking from nerves.

Christie looked at Katie. Correction: Christie devoured Katie with her eyes. And then she smiled without showing her perfectly veneered teeth and said, "Well, got to go! Toodles!" and she spun around and left. I knew she couldn't wait to get out of eyeshot so she could start the gossip mill churning.

I looked at Katie, embarrassed. "I'm sorry about that. She's . . ."

"She's hilarious! Oh my God! 'Toodles'?! She's, like, straight out of a movie!" Katie hayucked and I just looked at her, amused. I guess I was used to obnoxious people like Christie Billingsgate. I couldn't help but laugh along at Katie's enjoyment.

"Pretty ridiculous, huh?"

"Amazing!" Katie said. "I can't even believe you *know* people like that, Bobbo! I *love* it!" We laughed some more and then sipped our iced tea and got back to the subject at hand. "Okay," she said, putting some artificial sweetener into her drink, "so, I'm out, huh? When did the decree come down?"

"Well, it's nothing personal, Katie. Ava really likes you, it's just—"

"Stop it, Bobbo. It's totally fine. I *so* get it."

"You do? You know, you're amazing, Katie. You really are."

"No! You guys are! It's been an incredible couple of weeks. I've been feeling like *such* a princess, but I totally get it. Your wife wants her life and her family and her husband back!"

"That's all, Katie. It's nothing personal. I hope you know that."

"I know, I know."

"Anyway, I'm leaving for my big trip with Dicky next Saturday, and you should stay until then."

"Ohhhh, that is *so* great, Bobbo. Seriously. So nice. I'll totally be able to find a place by then."

"And you know what? If you need a little loan to help you get into a place or anything, I'd be absolutely delighted to do that."

"Oh, Bobbo. You're the best." She reached across and put her hand on mine again and then came over and gave me a kiss on the cheek and a long hug and for a second I closed my eyes and smelled her familiar smell and enjoyed the moment. And then I snapped out of it and gently pushed her away. I couldn't help but feel like the whole world was watching.

CHAPTER

Ten

August 31, 2001. The night before Dicky and I were leaving for our camping trip. Katie's last night in the house.

Dinner.

Me, Ava, Katie, Jack.

This had become a somewhat typical scenario over the past few weeks, but tonight was different. There was no tension.

Just the four of us.

Some wine. Some music.

We were eating dinner outside in the backyard, at a table on the deck. Jack was sleeping happily in a bassinet next to the table. It was a warm night with no breeze. I barbequed some steaks and some chicken. I'd been working on perfecting ribs on the barbeque and that night I'd burned an entire rack to an inedible crisp. Katie was moving out in the morning, and for the first time in weeks, Ava was in a genuinely good mood. We had just polished off an excellent bottle of pinot noir, and in a surprise turn, Katie declared that she was going to have some wine with us and there was nothing we could do about it. I didn't feel good about her break from sobriety but she said she wouldn't take no for an answer and what could I do to stop her? The two girls, a little bit buzzed and giddy, were making fun of my lackluster skills on the barbeque.

"Most people make baby *back* ribs, my husband makes baby *black* ribs," Ava said after swallowing a sip of wine. Katie cackled.

"Look on the bright side, though, you can use those ribs as charcoal next time you barbeque!" said Katie. And they both laughed some more. I was feeling pretty high and lighthearted at the moment, so I just watched the two of them yuk it up with a smile on my face.

"You two are like Abbott and friggin' Costello, lemme tell you," I said.

"Oh c'mon, honey," said Ava. "Abbott and Costello? That's, like, *so* something my *dad* would say! What's next, a Howdy Doody joke?"

"Oh, excuuuuuuse me!" I said, mock-offended. "I didn't realize the Reference Police would be out tonight!"

Ava started making siren sounds and twirling her finger around in the air. "You're under arrest!" she said, thrusting that pointed finger at me, to more giggling from Katie.

"Okay, okay, you two," I said as I rose from my chair. "I'm sayin' uncle. I'll go in and get dessert."

"Go ahead, you old fogy! We'll be out here instructing your son not to take barbeque lessons from his daddy."

As I walked toward the house I could hear the two women chatting and laughing behind me and it made me smile. I was thinking about how this had all worked out okay after all. Maybe Katie could even come over and have dinner with us every once in a while. So I'd had a rough couple of weeks, big deal. I did a good deed and my wife would get over it and the slate would be wiped clean starting tomorrow.

I went into the kitchen and unboxed the apple pie that Ava had brought home. As I moved toward the back door I realized how much better the pie would be with some vanilla ice cream and went into the freezer to look for some but there wasn't any there. I went out the back door with some new ammo to use against my relentlessly mocking wife.

When Ava saw me coming she said, "Wait until you guys try this pie. It is the most amazing thing in the universe."

"You know what would make it even more amazing?" I asked with a loaded look at Ava.

She knew I was getting at something and her eyes went wide. "Oh no. Tell me I forgot to buy vanilla ice cream. No, no, no, noooooo."

"You forgot to buy vanilla ice cream. Yes, yes, yes, yessssss," I said, enjoying my minor victory.

"Shit!" she said.

"It's okay, honey," I said. "We can eat it without ice cream. I'm just busting your chops."

"No, no, no. You know what, I have to go out anyway to buy milk for Jack. I was gonna go later, but I'll just run out now and get both at the corner store. Can you guys wait ten minutes for dessert?"

"I can definitely wait," Katie said. "I'm still full from dinner."

"I'll go, honey, " I volunteered, trying to be the hero.

"No! I'll get it!" Ava insisted. "*I'm* the one who forgot to get it in the first place."

"Are you sure?" I asked. "Are you sober enough to drive?"

"Are you kidding?" Ava asked. "I'm *fine*! I had *one* glass! I'm *so* fine."

And I let her go.

I let her go.

Ava left and Katie and I sat there and stared at each other for a couple of seconds. We swirled our wine in our glasses and then we both took sips.

"So this is it, huh, Bobbo?"

"This is it," I said, raising my glass in the air. She did the same and we air-clinked.

"Our last time alone," she said. The flirty nature of her remark surprised me, and I felt a little stirring in my boxer shorts. She smiled in a way that could've been seductive . . . or she may have been joking. I wasn't sure.

"Oh, stop it," I said, and I smiled, too.

"I'm gonna miss you, Bobbo."

"I'm gonna miss you, too, kid. It was fun having you here."

"It was fun being here." She stopped and thought about what to say next. "You know, I'm really proud of the man you turned into."

"Thanks, Katie. And even though you're drinking right now," I said with a grin and a disapproving wag of my pointer finger, "I'm awfully proud of you, too. You've really turned your life around and I think that's wonderful."

And then she said something that I would obsess about years later. "I wish . . . I wish there could be a happy ending for everyone." She gulped, and looked up at the sky. "It's gonna get dark soon," she said, unaware at just how prescient that observation would turn out to be. Just then the CD that we'd been listening to abruptly ended. We stared at each other. It looked like she was looking at my mouth. I was staring at her roving eyes and her flawless skin. I could've stared at Katie Turner for hours.

Katie smiled. "Awkward silence!"

"I'll go put on another CD."

"'Kay," she said.

"Be *right* back." I did a shuffle-jog toward the back door of the house. I went inside and into the living room where the sound system was located and opened its dark wood cabinet. I couldn't help but think about how adorable Katie was and how she had definitely just been flirting with me back there and it made me feel kind of studly. *Man, marriage really is a constant test,* I thought.

I chose Paul Simon's *Graceland,* and put it into the CD player. I stood up and turned around.

And there she was.

I hadn't heard her come in. She was standing inches from me. We were practically eye to eye. She glanced down at my mouth again. Bit her lower lip very slightly. And I knew what was about to happen. But it couldn't possibly happen. I'd never let it happen.

And then it happened.

She kissed me.

Very gently at first, like the flutter of a tiny feather, her lips on mine. I froze in place. I closed my eyes and it felt like the most pleasant of dreams. And then I lost control. Her mouth was open now and so was mine and I could taste the wine on her and then her soft, delicious tongue was tangled with mine and I was lost in the moment and before I knew it I was kissing her back. Hard. Her lips were full and soft and her tongue was warm and wet and welcoming. She put her hand on the back of my head and I could feel her fingernails caressing my scalp and I reached up and dug my hand under her soft, heavy hair and felt her head in my hand and we kissed and kissed. Deep and hard and hungry.

And then I came to and realized what was going on and that it was real and it was happening and I hit the brakes. I pulled away.

"I can't—," I said.

"I'm sorry," she said, brushing her lips with the back of her hand. "Oh God, Bobbo, I'm so sorry. I shouldn't've—"

"It's okay."

"No, oh gosh." She looked down and put her hand to her forehead now.

"Katie, it's okay. Don't worry. It's . . . it's okay." It

really wasn't okay but I didn't know what else to say. "Ava should be back soon . . ." I looked at my watch.

"Oh my God. That was so wrong. I'm sorry, Bobbo. I really thought—Oh God. I made this *so* awkward. Oh my God. This is terrible."

"No, no. Katie. It's fine."

We looked at each other. We were still standing pretty close. Katie swallowed hard. I did, too. She looked up at me with an "Oops!" sort of expression on her face. In that moment I remember thinking that if I didn't tell Ava about this I would never be able to sleep again.

"God, Bobbo, you look like you just saw a ghost!"

"Well"—I scratched my chin and considered that—"I kinda did." She laughed and gave my chest a slap and let her hand linger there for a second and even though we were done kissing, I felt like we were still in danger of being busted by Ava at any moment and I suddenly felt very exposed and vulnerable and of course that was when Ava walked in.

"Ava!" I said, taking an involuntary step back from Katie.

Ava looked at us and her head cocked ever so slightly to the side and maybe it was my imagination but I could swear the most fleeting look of curious indignation passed across her face, before she held up a plastic bag and forced a smile and said, "Ice cream's here!"

"Excellent!" I said, trying to act my most normal.

"What're you guys doing?" Ava asked, now without any apparent recrimination.

"We were changing the CD," I said, pointing up at the sky as if that were where the music was coming from.

"*Graceland*!" Katie said.

"Ooh, good choice, you guys!" said Ava, and I couldn't tell if we were all just standing here pretending like this was a normal conversation, or if it was actually passing for a normal conversation. Paul Simon was singing something about these being the days of miracle and wonder and "don't cry, baby, don't cry, don't cry . . ." and that was when I thought about Jack, outside all by himself.

"I'll go out to the baby. Why don't you guys get dessert all set and bring it out."

They both headed toward the kitchen. My head was spinning. I headed toward the backyard and the end of my life as I knew it.

CHAPTER
Eleven

I've died a million times.

Every time I think about what came next, I die again.

And again.

And again.

The walk out to the backyard.

In the wake of the kiss with Katie, the utter betrayal of my marriage I had just committed, my heart was already hammering as I crossed the threshold to the outside of the house.

My thoughts were moving a million miles a minute as I approached the bassinet in which Jack slept. *What have I done?* I thought. *How am I going to live with this?*

The bassinet faced away from me, and we'd draped a blanket over the hood to block the setting sun from shining on Jack, and also to give him some measure of peace while we were chatting.

I grabbed the handles of the bassinet, and bowed my head. I gently rocked it a few times, thinking about what'd just happened, before realizing that Jack was already asleep, and my rocking might wake him.

It didn't matter.

I took a deep breath and told myself that I'd have to play it cool for a bit. *I shouldn't tell her now. She's finally back to her old self.*

None of it mattered.

I walked around the bassinet and lifted up the blanket to check on Jack.

I grabbed the corner of the blanket.

Folded it back.

Jack

was

gone.

CHAPTER
Twelve

I ripped the blanket off the hood of the bassinet.

My son was not in there.

We had left him alone outside for approximately five minutes.

Five minutes.

And he was gone.

My infant son.

Disappeared. Vanished.

Not possible, but there it was.

Gone.

I tore through the pillows and blankets in his bassinet, my heart exploding. "Jack?" I said, though it was clear he wasn't there. I stood up and looked around. My brain couldn't compute what was happening. I felt like a skipping record.

My head whipped around the backyard. Where could

he have gone? I immediately became aware of hundreds of vulnerable spots along the fence and tree line where someone could get in. Parts of our yard I had never considered before I was now analyzing at a billion images per second. I tried to glimpse movement between the trees in the thicket that surrounded the yard. I ran to one side of the deck, grabbing the railing and looking out at the woods behind my house, like I was on a boat and my child had been washed overboard. "Jack?!" I had a lump in my throat the size of a grapefruit. I couldn't hear a thing. No crying, no nothing. I saw no signs of life out there. And then I heard the back door open and just as it did I couldn't help but let out a wail and the last thing I remember hearing was the echo of my scream and Ava saying my name quietly and our dessert plates hitting the wooden deck.

CHAPTER

Thirteen

How do I tell this part of the story?

How do I express in words what we went through in those next moments? Those excruciating next hours and days? How can I relive it? How does one articulate pain and shock and loss like this?

No one can begin to understand.

We frantically searched the small grove of trees behind our house. My hands were scratched and bloodied from tearing through the brambles. I remember hearing Ava screaming and crying into the phone that our baby had been kidnapped. I remember seeing Katie with makeup-stained tears streaming down her face, ripping through the brush a few feet from me, calling Jack's name.

I ran down the street.

I screamed his name.

I pounded on doors.

I screamed his name.

We all screamed his name.

The police arrived.

We were frantic.

They asked questions.

They promised to put together a search party immediately.

Put out an APB.

They tried to calm us down.

We were uncalmable.

I got in my car and I drove.

Katie tried to stop me but that was not possible.

There were flashlights and distressed expressions.

I drove and I cried and I called his name out the window as if he were a runaway dog that would come back when I beckoned.

People stared from their front lawns.

I went home to the circus.

The police and the media and our friends. *How did the media get there so quickly?*

They took photos and they shined lights and shouted questions.

Dicky was there. He helped me inside.

The Ava I'd known went into the kitchen to prepare dessert and never came back. This was the ghost of Ava. Pale and thin and unable to communicate.

We sat rigidly on separate chairs in the living room like cadavers. Ava and I. Katie. Dicky. Several police officers and whoever else. We lay slumped there. Silent. Like sculptures in some morbid statuary.

What else could we do?

Eleven days apparently went by like this. I don't know what we did in that time. I don't know if we ate or bathed or slept or left the house. This is the only image I have of those days. Sitting in that room.

People coming and going.

We did a press conference that I don't remember.

The police telling us they were still looking. No traces of Jack.

A fruitless manhunt.

Friends and relatives passing through like shit through a goose.

Trying to comfort the un-comfortable.

And then, eleven days after my son Jack vanished from under my nose, on Tuesday, September 11th, 2001, two planes crashed into the World Trade Center.

And the world forgot all about my son.

CHAPTER

Fourteen

Tragedy happens every single day. Sure, there are different levels and degrees of calamity and suffering, and in scope and breadth the cataclysmic events of 9/11 certainly dwarfed what would seem in comparison to be less substantial incidents, but that doesn't make these other incidents less important; less tragic; less of a priority. Life, merciless and brutal, pressed on for those of us not directly connected to the 9/11 tragedy. Ava and I were floored by the terrorist attacks as much as everyone else, but our prior devastation did not vanish into the ether. We couldn't put our troubles aside and count our blessings and hold our neighbors' hands and unite as flag-waving Americans in our time of national crisis.

What about *us? Our son had been kidnapped!*

No one talks about the *other* stuff that happened on or around 9/11. The normal, pitiless drumbeat of life that ceaselessly droned on in the background of the national tragedy, unheard like music in a crashing elevator. What about all the fathers who had heart attacks that day? The teenagers in fatal car accidents? The kidney transplants that didn't happen? The infants that were kidnapped from their parents' backyards while their dads were supposed to be watching them?

They didn't get any airtime.

Before we knew it Ava and I were alone.

No more cops. No more media. No more friends. Everyone had a bigger nightmare to contend with now.

At some point, Katie excused herself from our house, unnoticed. Packed her bags and scooted out the door. Dicky left, too, but not before thoroughly medicating us with Valium and Xanax and morphine and OxyContin.

We were alone, save for pill bottles and silence.

A few days after 9/11, I moved around the house. I began to eat a little bit. I showered.

Ava was a shell.

A shadow.

Vapor.

Practically indiscernible.

She seemed to never move from the couch. She watched the news coverage of the terrorist attacks, unblinking and unemotional.

I started to feel like we were specters, silent and tortured, haunting the house that we'd once lived in.

At some point, after what seemed like weeks of complete radio silence, the police called and told us they hadn't found anything yet, but they assured us that they were still looking. I didn't feel assured.

And then, fourteen days after Jack had disappeared, Ava spoke to me.

I'd finally dragged her off of the couch, away from the television, and up to our bedroom. She hadn't slept in our bed in fourteen nights. I wrapped a robe around her and escorted her upstairs. She felt like a frail elderly person. Like she'd somehow aged fifty years in two weeks. We didn't speak the whole way up. I eased her into bed, pulled the covers up over her.

I went around to my side of the bed and sat down on its edge. I took my watch off and rubbed my face with both hands. I massaged my temples. I peeled back the covers and got into bed next to the ghost of my wife. I clicked off the bedside lamp.

We lay in silence for a long time.

And then, from the darkness came a question. "What were you doing, Bobby?"

I didn't know what she meant. This was the first she'd spoken in weeks.

She didn't say anything else.

I wasn't sure if she was asleep or awake.

In the middle of the night, I sat up in bed when I realized the meaning of her question.

I wasn't the only one who held myself responsible.

I wept.

CHAPTER
Fifteen

Ava could no longer look at me.

The love of my life could not bear the sight of my face.

I wondered what was going on in her mind. Did she suspect that something had happened between Katie and me while she was out getting ice cream? Is that what she'd meant by her question? Is this what she'd been doing in her silence? Analyzing the events in her head, indicting me and finding me guilty? Was it more loaded than a simple "Why weren't you watching him?" Did it matter? I don't know. What definitely mattered was that Jack had disappeared when I was supposed to be with him. Guarding him. Protecting him. Being a good father. This is what mattered to Ava, and this is what mattered to me.

My wife couldn't look at me, because every time she did, she saw the man who lost her child.

I couldn't blame her. This was who I saw in the mirror, too. Only I saw the more despicable, unspeakable version. The version that was kissing another woman while he should have been sitting inches from his son. This act of adultery added exponential guilt to my shoulders. How could I live with myself? How could I function?

Pills and whisky, that's how.

Lots of pills, and lots of whisky.

I'd never been much of a drinker, and certainly not a drug user, but it seemed the only way to dull the agony.

After almost a month of being locked in the house with a silent Ava, Dicky convinced me that I should try to come into the office. I didn't want to be around anyone. I didn't want to see the pity and concern written all over their faces. I didn't want to hear how they were praying for us. I didn't want to deal, period. But he was right. I needed to get out of the house.

But could I leave Ava alone?

I called her friend Christie. She agreed to come and keep Ava company while I was at the office.

I started going to work again. I stayed in my private office. I did paperwork and other mindless stuff. I didn't see patients. I popped pills. I took tugs off hidden whisky bottles.

It was only one week. Not *even* one week. I'd started going to work on Monday, and this was Thursday. It was a half day. A morning. I got to my office at around nine, and left around three. But sure enough, when I got home, Ava was gone.

CHAPTER
Sixteen

It's unfathomable how such a small thing can lead to such a large thing. If I had never gotten that IM from Katie Turner, the chain of events that led to us kissing in my living room would never have happened. I wouldn't have left my infant son outside all by himself.

Life is a mean-spirited cocksucker.

Ava wouldn't take my calls. Finally, after two days of incessantly calling her cell phone, Christie answered to give me the bad news. "It's over, Bobby. She can't stand to be around you right now. It's too painful."

That was it. From the mouth of Christie Fucking Billingsgate.

Glug glug glug goes the whisky.

She can't stand to be around you right now. What the hell did that mean? Did she blame me entirely for Jack's disappearance? Did she know about the kiss? Or was it simply that I reminded her too much of what she'd lost?

Truth be told, I didn't blame her for leaving. I couldn't fight it. I felt I was getting what I deserved.

It was really no quieter in the house with Ava gone. We hadn't spoken in over a month, anyway.

But it felt different.

Now I'd lost the two people in the world who were most important to me. Four people, if you count my parents. What else did I have? I had nothing to live for but the hope that my son would return to me. And maybe if Jack came back, Ava would, too. All my friends seemed to have vanished as well. Sure, when we were a hot news story everyone wanted to be involved. But now that I was a pariah (at least in my own mind), where did everybody go?

I called the police detective assigned to our case.

His exact words were, "I don't want you to think we don't have our eyes wide open for your boy, because we do, but with all that is going on in the world, and with how long it's been since he disappeared, I also want you to understand that the chances of finding him at this point are next to nil. But yeah, *of course* we're still looking."

Oh yeah, of course.

Pills, pills, pills.

Dicky was trying to keep me centered. Keep a routine going. I started to see patients on a very limited basis. Only my most loyal, because they insisted.

People looked at me funny, and I wondered, *Do they know I'm so high on pills I can barely tell their knees from their elbows? Or are they looking at me because they know the truth about what happened? Do they know that I am responsible for losing my son and destroying my family?*

I soon noticed that even my most loyal patients were seeing Dicky instead of me. I saw their scared looks when I walked into the waiting room, like, "Oh no, please don't call my name. Not the guy who lost his kid. I don't want him touching *my* kid."

I was drinking myself into a coma every night. I stumbled around in a pill-induced blur every day. I was spiraling, to say the least. I thought about my father a lot during this time. How easy it would be to choose his way out.

I reached out to Katie Turner at some point, but the cell phone number she'd been using before had been disconnected. Her emails bounced back to me, too. I wondered how the tragedy had affected her, and I hoped she was okay. I hoped it hadn't sent her stumbling back down a bad path.

It was also around this time that I first noticed this little black dog hanging around. Sometimes I'd see him on my street. And then sometimes I'd see him out and about town. And then one day he showed up in the parking lot of my office. I got out of my car and we stared at each other.

"Hey, buddy," I said to the dog. He didn't react.

I bent down to his level. "You following me, doggy? I've seen you around town." He stared at me and cocked his head. "How you doing, pal?"

I reached out a hand for him to sniff, and he hesitantly approached and sniffed. I ventured a rub between his ears. He dug it. He was a mutt. He looked like a black Lab, only smaller and with the wiry, spiky hair of a terrier.

I assumed he was a stray, because I'd seen him around town all by himself a handful of times now, but I was surprised to see that up close, he was clean and fat and his coat was shiny. He didn't have a collar. He had these beautiful, expressive light brown eyes. He loved the attention I gave him. After petting and whispering to him for a few minutes I stood and walked toward my office, beckoning him to follow, and he did. I figured I'd take him inside and give him some water. He followed me right up to the steps of the office and stopped. "Come on, Bud!" I called, but he wouldn't come up the stairs, no matter how politely I asked. So I went inside. I got a bowl of water, and I brought it out to him. But when I came back, he was gone.

I shrugged it off and went into my office. I sat down and started to sort through some paperwork. About twenty minutes later, I heard a dog barking. I went to the window. And there he was. Sitting outside of my office, panting away, looking right at me.

This was certainly a little weird. Black Lassie was stalking me.

I went outside again with the bowl of water. I walked around to the side of the building where my window was. No dog.

"Flopster!"

I turned to see Dicky strutting from his car to the office.

"What you doin' out here?" he asked.

"I saw a stray dog out here from my window, so I came to check it out, maybe give it some water, but he's gone."

"Oh? Okay. Come on back inside, okay? You can help me with some stuff." I could hear the condescension in

Dicky's voice. It had been there for the last few weeks, a light varnish on the woodwork of our fragile conversations. I knew he was nervous about my rapidly degrading behavior. Once or twice over the past weeks he'd casually cautioned me to be careful taking pills during work hours. "No biggie. Just, you know, keep an eye on it."

As we walked toward the front door of our office, he put his arm around me. "How you feelin', Flop?" Loaded, pointed question.

"How do you think I'm feelin', *Dick*?" I asked. He looked surprised by my tone. He removed his arm from around my shoulder.

"You been drinking, Bobby?" Like he didn't know how fucked up I'd been every second of every day for the last few months. Like he hadn't been party to it. This rubbed me wrong. Very wrong.

"What do you think, Dick? You think maybe I've been drinking, Detective? You're pretty observant. You should be a fucking PI in your spare time."

"Floppy. Don't do this. Listen to me. I love you."

"Yeah?"

"Stop it. You're drunk. You reek. Just go home. Let me call you a cab."

I stared him in the eyes. I was annoyed, but not quite drunk enough to get belligerent. I didn't want to fight with the guy. He was my best friend and he meant well. And really, he was right. I was drunk.

I went inside, packed my stuff, and left the office. And just as I stepped into the parking lot, there was the dog again. Sitting by my car, as if he were waiting for me to punch out and go for a beer with him.

Weird little pooch.

I approached him and he let me bend down and scratch his head again, and I thought, *At least there's someone in the world who wants to be around me. Maybe I can take this li'l fella home. I could certainly use the company.* So I took a few steps toward my car and he followed. As soon as I opened the back door he jumped right in. I suddenly felt like I was under surveillance, but when I looked around, there seemed to be no one watching. I got in the car, and drove home with my new friend.

I stopped en route to pick up steaks for me and Bob Barker. That's what I decided to call him. Bob Barker. Always wanted to name a dog that. So I barbequed some nice eight-ounce filets mignon for me and my new pal Bob Barker. I poured a little of my beer in a bowl for him and we enjoyed a manly dinner together and watched *SportsCenter*. Bob Barker was a Dodgers fan and I was a Yankees fan, but we got along just fine.

After a few beers, a few Percocets (none for Bob Barker), and a few more beers, we got to talking. Well, I got to talking, anyway. Bob Barker was a very good listener. I told him the whole story. "And now I got nothin', Bob. I got this empty house. I got these baby toys. I've got a lot of pills and a lot of grief and I've got an empty bed upstairs. I got no one and I got nothing." Bob Barker totally sympathized.

"You got me, Bobby," he seemed to say with his big brown eyes.

CHAPTER
Seventeen

Bob Barker and I hung out a bunch more times. Some days he would be outside my office when I got off work. Sometimes I'd see him on the street while driving, and I'd pick him up. Once he was even at my house when I got home! I cherished our strange relationship.

A few weeks after my "conversation" with Dicky about my drinking at the office, the situation came to a head. It was a Thursday morning in early February. Dicky and I had had a run-in the evening before when I'd hobbled out of the office, fucked up on a couple of Vicodins. He'd offered to drive me home and I told him to fuck off, right in front of several patients.

I was very drunk when I got to the office at 9:30 a.m. on this particular day. I hadn't even gotten into my bed the night before, and I hadn't changed my clothes from the previous day—both habits that were becoming more and more common. Bob Barker was in the parking lot of my office when I got there. I was glad to see him. It had been a few days.

I stumbled over to the steps at the entrance of our office, and plopped down on the second step. I was petting Bob Barker and talking softly to him when Dicky approached. I hadn't heard him coming, and he startled me when he said my name.

"Hey," I said, blinking away the sunlight that haloed him, using my hand as a visor.

"What are you doing, Bobby?" Dicky asked.

"I'm petting the dog, man."

"What dog, Bobby?"

Sure enough, when I looked down at the spot where Bob Barker had been lying just a moment before, he was gone.

Dicky looked at me like I was batshit crazy. I took a deep breath and tried to play it cool. "Shit, well, there *was* a dog here a minute ago, man. You must've scared him off. You scared me, too."

Dicky stared at me, his face full of concern. "C'mon, pal. Let's go inside. I'll buy you breakfast."

He helped me up and we entered the office together. The waiting room was full. Lots of "Good morning, Docs!" as we made our way through to our respective offices. Dicky asked one of the receptionists to go grab us a few breakfast burritos and coffees from a place down the street that we both liked.

As we arrived at my office, Dicky stopped on his way to his own office and asked, "You okay, Flop?"

I said I was.

"Let's have breakfast together when the food gets here, 'kay?"

"'Kay," I said, knowing that my pre-breakfast would consist of a few Xanax and a couple of tugs of Johnnie Walker. As soon as I got to my desk I did just that. By the time our food arrived I was a complete disaster. I misjudged just how much four Xanax would mess me up. I was drifting merrily merrily merrily down the stream toward REM sleep while sitting up at my desk when my intercom buzzed and Dicky said, "Flop—food's here." Messed up as I was, I knew this wasn't going to go well. But I was feeling pretty floaty at that point, and I didn't care.

I teeter-tottered my way into his office. I could feel people looking at me. Nurses and receptionists and patients.

Didn't care.

When I got there, Dicky wasn't alone. Our other partner, the older doctor who'd started our practice with us years prior, Dr. Tobias Stenzler, was sitting in one of the two chairs on the other side of Dicky's desk. They both looked at me with worry in their eyes. I couldn't help but smile.

"Uh-ohhhh! Principal's office for meeeee!" I said. "I'm in trouuuuuble!"

"Please sit, Robert," said Stenzler.

"Heh. Robert. Yes, occifer!" I said with a proper military salute. I slammed the door, pirouetted, and stumbled over to the empty chair. I almost missed, but I managed to get my butt into the seat.

It was quiet for a minute. I stared at Dicky, who looked down at his desk. I was thinking that he was a total fucking stranger. I barely recognized him anymore. Not to mention Stenzler, whose name I could barely recall.

I stared at Dicky and thought about what this asshole might be about to say to me. It didn't take a doctor to figure out where this conversation was headed. I hated Dicky at that moment. Arrogant, self-righteous prick. He was the one who'd prescribed me these pills in the first place. Dicky squished his mouth up into a pucker and moved his little cocky puckered mouth from side to side. "We can't do this anymore, Flop."

I tooted a laugh through my nose.

"I'm serious. You know no one cares about you more than I do. But this is a real problem. We've tolerated it for a long time now because of everything you've been through. But this is a doctor's office. Look at you. You're a mess. We could all lose our licenses."

"Oh, this is a doctor's office? Fuck you, Dick."

"Floppy, come on. Don't do that."

"Quit calling me *Floppy*. It's condescending."

"Bobby, I've been researching rehab facilities and—"

"Oh, fuck off—"

Stenzler chimed in, "This is a very serious liability, Robert—"

"SHUT THE FUCK UP, *TOBIAS*," I hissed. This quieted the both of them. I liked it.

Finally, Dicky said, "Bobby, he's right. People are talking."

"Ohhhhh! People are talking, are they? Talking about

the biiiiig liability! The Good Doctor Bobby who lost his kid! Lost his wife! Bad for business! Right, Dick?" It was pretty fun being able to call him a dick under the guise of his name. I stormed to the door and tore it open.

"Bobby—"

"Wouldn't want to cramp your style, hotshot! Hurt the bottom line!"

"Floppy, come on, stop it."

"Don't 'FLOPPY' me, cocksucker! You're not my fuckin' boss!" The ol' you're-not-the-boss-of-me angle. Very mature and effective.

We were now officially making a scene. Okay, *I* was officially making a scene. The waiting room was only a few steps down a short hallway.

Dicky stood up and moved toward me. I think he only meant to close the door so the whole office wouldn't hear us (me). But he got too close and I was on the defensive and I took a swing. I took a swing at Dicky. My partner and my best friend.

I didn't come close.

In fact, I almost fell on my face following through with the punch. To protect himself he bear-hugged me from behind and then when I flailed at him, he gave me a shove to put some distance between us. I tripped over my own feet and fell hard into the hallway and crumpled as I hit the spot where the wall met the floor.

I looked up at him and Stenzler, who stood in the doorway looking down at me. It was one of the darker moments of my life, and one of the last things I can remember before a long period of haze.

I looked in the other direction, down the hallway,

and saw the whole waiting room staring at me. I tried to pick myself up off the ground. It took me a pitifully long time. All I could think was, *GO*. When I finally managed to get to my feet, I made a wobbly break for the exit, but as I bumbled and tripped down the hallway, through the waiting room, and toward the front door, I fell. And this wasn't like the last fall. There was no wall there to stop me this time. This time I was in the waiting room. The waiting room of a pediatrician's office. Full of children. I fell hard. With some speed and weight propelling me.

And as I dropped I landed on a five-year-old boy named Jordan Coulter, shattering his humerus, his radius, his ulna, and his wrist in one fell swoop.

Shit, meet fan.

CHAPTER

Eighteen

I don't want to beat a dead horse here. I've made it utterly clear that I was very messed up on booze and
pills. But all of that was just foreplay.

The front-page story of the *Los Angeles Times* the
next morning was "More Troubles for Tragic Doc." The
subhead read, "MD in Mourning Injures Child Patient
in Alcohol and Drug-fueled incident."

I was a headline again. The reporters materialized
in front of my house. It brought our whole story back
to the front page. Stirred up all the sediment that had
finally begun to settle.

I was all kinds of messed up.

The day after the "incident" my phone rang off
the hook. I vaguely remember voice mail messages
from my lawyer, someone else's lawyer, the Medical Board of California, another lawyer, Dicky, Ava's

lawyer, some reporters . . . I don't remember who else.

The summary of said messages: my license to practice medicine in the state of California was suspended until further review, I was being sued by the family of young Jordan Coulter, I was asked to not come to the office for a while, Dicky wanted to put me in rehab, and Ava officially filed for a divorce.

I truly can't tell you what happened or how long it took to happen. I have swatches of memory. But they are incomplete snapshots, like Polaroid pictures that didn't quite develop right. They're yellow and blurred and covered in light flares.

One such image shows me leaning over on my couch and vomiting on the living room floor, one arm on the coffee table, my doorbell ringing incessantly. My phone ringing. There's a TV on somewhere and they are talking about 9/11.

Another snapshot shows Ava standing in the foyer of our house, arms crossed over her chest, with a man in a suit standing next to her looking very serious. They're telling me that "the deal" I signed requires that I evacuate the premises and turn the house over to her immediately. *The deal I signed?* News to me.

One shot shows my mustached lawyer, Charlie Walter, and a woman I don't recognize helping me out of the house and into a car that I also don't recognize.

One shows a view from the bed of a plushly appointed bedroom that I am unfamiliar with. The ceiling above the bed has a hairline crack in it, the shape of which alternately resembles the state of Florida and an uncircumcised penis. Someone hands me some pills and I swallow them without water.

That's all I got.

I woke up on a cold floor.

I had no idea where I was or how long I'd been there. The floor was beautiful brownish stone, highly polished. I was in a bathroom. There was shit in my pants and dried vomit on my shirt.

There was a staccato *click-click-clicking* in my head.

Clickclick . . . CLICK . . . click . . . clack . . . CLICK-CLICKCLICK . . . Little tapdancers dancing around my skull.

This was weird.

I felt as if someone had thrown sand in my eyes. I could barely swallow. It was like my mouth was filled with acrid, dried-up honey.

Let me back up a second: there was shit in my pants.

Reaching up to a nearby counter for stability, I managed to gather up my creaking and achy bones, and pull myself up off the floor. I leaned over the sink and turned on the water. I made a conscious decision—my first in God knows how long—to *not* look at myself in the mirror. The sticker on the plastic wrap clinging to the soap in the soap dish told me that I was at a place called Shutters on the Beach. Somewhere in my brain I recalled that this was one of the nicest hotels in Santa Monica.

Super. Now where are my fucking pills?

And also, there is shit in my pants and that, too, should make the TO-DO list.

But first things first. The cold water did absolutely nothing to clear my head. I stumbled out of the bathroom into a beautiful suite. The curtains were drawn, and thank the Lord, it was very dark. Music played from a clock radio. "Take Me Home Tonight," by Eddie Money. Wonderful irony. The clicking in my head was incessant and crazy-making. I futilely banged on my skull to try to knock it out. My vision was screwed up. I kept seeing very brief flashes where everything in the room appeared to be white. The walls, the furniture, everything. Bleached white. I spotted two large suitcases in a corner of the room, at the foot of the curtains. I blinked once and they were gone. Blinked again and there they were. I recognized that they were mine, though I didn't know how they got there or what they contained. I dug through them.

They were full of my belongings. Stuff from my house. Mostly clothing. I also found the little blue stuffed bear that I'd bought for Jack in the hospital on the day he was born. I removed that from the bag, put it to my nose, and inhaled. Then I frantically looked for my toiletry kit, and found it. No pills.

Clickety-CLICK. Click click click click click. CLACK! Like a typewriter going off right next to both of my ears.

Fuck, that's annoying!

My attention was drawn to a blinking light on the telephone on the nightstand. My wallet, watch, and cell phone were also there. And lo and behold, whatever wise and altruistic saint was kind enough to pack up my shit and get me here was benevolent and/or stupid enough to put several of my more valuable prescriptions right there next to the bed. I put the little blue teddy bear down on the nightstand. I popped two OxyContin and went back to my bags to search for some booze. None in the suitcases. I went for the mini-bar.

Mini-jackpot. I downed two tiny bottles of tequila, a mini-bottle of whisky, and a mini-bottle of gin. I had no intention of checking the phone messages, but there was also a note on the beautiful wood and white-marble side table, which drew me back over there. The note, scribbled on hotel stationery, read:

ROBERT—WHEN YOU WAKE FROM YOUR STUPOR, CALL ME. I'LL EXPLAIN WHAT'S GOING ON SINCE YOU PROBABLY HAVE NO CLUE.

It was signed by my lawyer, Charlie Walter. *Charlie's a good guy. Always liked him,* I thought. *But I'm not ready to wake from my stupor. Sorry, Charlie.* I was, however, ready to get the shit from out of my pants and the CLICKing from out of my head.

I stripped off my jeans and my stink-filled under-wear, and put them both in a small plastic garbage bag that I pulled from the trash can in the bathroom. I tied the bag in a knot, and dropped it off of the bal-cony into the pool three stories below. This gave me a chuckle.

I returned to the mini-bar. There were five more mini-bottles of assorted liquor, four beers, a mini-bottle of champagne, and two mini-bottles of wine. I drank four of the remaining miniature bottles of liquor, and opened a beer to take into the shower with me. I turned the shower to scalding hot, and got in. I cleaned the shit and vomit off of my body, and as the OxyContin kicked in, I could only think of sleep. I sat down cross-legged on the shower floor (which was cool and wet and welcoming), took a swig of beer, and went to sleep.

CHAPTER

Nineteen

I was awakened sometime later (hours? days?) by loud, fevered chattering in an alien language. It was raining, and through the heavy fog I could see that there were two plump lavender and white extraterrestrials standing over me. I panicked for a moment, and then realized it wasn't fog or rain but very heavy steam and water from the shower. And they weren't extraterrestrials, but rather two squat, wide-faced Hispanic women wearing light-purple and white maid uniforms. They were machine-gunning at each other in rapid Spanish. They looked majorly freaked, but they didn't seem to notice, maybe because of the steam, that I was awake. One of them had a pink feather duster in her hand, which she held and shook at me like a magic wand. I looked down at my hands. My skin was so white and wrinkled it looked like it might shed like snakeskin.

"Ahh," I croaked.

This startled the maids, and they both yelped.

The one with the duster suddenly aimed her artillery gun mouth at me, and let loose with, "*¡AYYYY! ¡Señor! ¡Pensamos que usted era muerto! ¡Ayyyy, pobrecito! ¡Por favor! ¡Por favor! ¡Salga de la ducha antes de que usted dé vuelta en una pasa!*" She pointed her feather duster at me and waited for my response. I didn't respond because all I heard was, "*Babababababababababababababababa babababa.*"

I don't speak Spanish but I was pretty sure the loose translation was something along the lines of: "Get out of the shower, fucktard!"

They switched off the water, and, with shielded eyes so as not to see my shriveled man-parts, they helped me stand up. This wasn't so easy. I felt like I hadn't used my body in a very long time. They wrapped me in a plush white robe, and escorted me to the bed. My skin was hypersensitive and tender under the robe. The fabric seemed to have needles sticking out of it, pricking me all over.

I heard one of the maids barking at the other, "*¡Llame al doctor! ¡Rapidamente!*"

That I understood: Call the doctor. Quickly.

"No, no, no," I mumbled. I sounded as if a family of frogs had moved into my throat. "No *doctor*. No call *el doctor*. I *am* el doctor. Yo . . . soy . . . a . . . doctorrr." I knew I wasn't the most convincing guy in the world at the moment, considering the circumstances under which they'd just found me, but they seemed to be listening. "I'm okay," I pleaded. "I'm okay."

They looked at me, and at each other, and one of the little senoritas said to the other, *"Llame al abogado."* I didn't know what that meant, but I figured that a couple of pesos would probably get rid of them, so I grabbed for my wallet on the nearby desk, sliced off a couple of twenties, and ushered them out of the room before they knew what had happened.

My head was pounding. I felt weak and hot. I needed a drink. All that was left in the fridge was beer and wine and champagne. I pounded the bottle of champagne and one of the bottles of wine, but I needed something harder. I went for the phone. I pushed the room service button. I asked if it was possible to order full bottles of alcohol. They told me it *was* possible, but the overly helpful young lady intimated to me that the bottles were very expensive, and that I'd "prolllllllllly" be better off going to a local liquor store to purchase them myself at more reasonable prices. I told her to send up three bottles of whisky (at $350 a pop). She told me they'd be right up.

I fell back into bed. *Now what?*

I leaned over to the nightstand and popped an Oxy-Contin. I took a Xanax, too, just for shits and giggles. Now that I knew *where* I was I tried to figure out *when* I was. *What day is it? What is the last thing I can remember?*

It was quiet again, and the clicking sound returned.

CLACK CLACK click! Click clack click clack click clack.

And then my phone began to ring. I turned my head and stared at it, let it ring a few times while I decided what to do. The little blue bear was sitting there, next to the phone, looking at me. He didn't seem to care whether I answered the phone or not.

This is what the disheveled orchestra in my head sounded like:

Clickclickclick-RINNNNNNNNNNNNNG-click-CLACK-RINNNNN(click)NNNNNNNNG.

I decided that answering the phone would get rid of at least part of the cacophony, so I snatched it off the cradle.

"Yeah?" I croaked.

There was no response for a few seconds, and then: "Robert! Oh man! Hello? You there?" I didn't know who it was, but it sounded like he was calling from a walkie-talkie, or from far away, like maybe from another dimension.

"Yeah? Hello?" I said.

A delay. "Robert! Bob-Bobby! It's Charlie . . . Walter!" The line was staticky and there was a long delay between our responses. "He-hello? You there, Robert?"

"Yeah, I'm here. You calling me from the moon?"

Delay.

"Robert. Ha—the moon. I'm calling from St. Barths! Man, there's a terrible delay . . . Caribbean. Are you okay? I thought you'd never wake up! The maid finally called me . . ."

"The maid?" *Traitor.*

Delay.

"Yeah. Rufina. I paid her to check on you a few times a day and call me if you, I mean, she tells me *now* that she only works three days a week and hasn't been there since Wednesday, but—"

"Wuh-Wednesday? Is that a long—I mean how, uh, how long have I been here?"

Pause.

"You've been there for thirteen days, Robert."

Thirteen. Fucking. Days. Fuck.

"You shittin' me, Charlie?"

Delay.

"I shit you not, Bobby. I checked on you every day for the first week, but I, uh, I had this vacation planned with my family so I . . . you know, I felt terrible, Robert, but I had to, uh . . ."

I was starting to get anxiety from all the talking. "Tell me what's going on, Charlie. Please."

Delay.

"Oh. Yes. Of course. I don't know what you remember of the last month, Robert, because, uh, you know, you were pretty, uh . . . out of it, understandably, but here's the deal: You agreed—*insisted,* I should say—that Ava get the house and all of its contents." *Good,* I thought. *Woulda done that even if I'd been sober.* "You got to keep your car, which is parked in the valet lot at your hotel, and it's loaded with a bunch more of your belongings. Whatever Ava thought you'd want. Aside from the house, all of your assets have been divided in half. Okay?"

"What do I have?" I asked.

Delay.

"Well, all things considered, you're in good shape, Robert. In a nutshell, the sum total of your assets as of today, including the value of all stocks and bonds and funds, and all liquid in various savings and checking

125

accounts, after giving Ava half, is one hundred thirty-six thousand four hundred twenty-four dollars and sixty-seven cents. I would recom—"

"That's all I needed to hear, Charlie. Please liquidate everything I have and put it into my checking account."

A delay. Longer than the previous ones.

"Liquidate everything, Robert? Are you su—"

"Yes, Charlie. I'm sure. Do it."

Delay.

"Okay, but, uh—"

"Thanks, Charlie." I hung up the phone.

A hundred forty grand could keep me highly sedated in this hotel room for the foreseeable future.

I stared at the uncircumcised penis crack in the ceiling. To stop the clicking I turned on the television and watched a few minutes of a *Family Feud* rerun before I fell asleep. The contestants at the podium were those two little Mexican maids in their lavender and white uniforms. As I floated off to Dreamland, I thought, *Well that's odd.*

CHAPTER

Twenty

Charlie Walter returned from the Caribbean at some point.

I woke up one morning and there he was, standing next to my bed.

I thought it was a few days later, but he told me that two weeks had gone by.

"You don't look well, Robert," Charlie said through his mustache and sunburn.

I looked up at him but had no reasonable response. I was sure he was right. I wasn't showering or shaving or brushing my teeth anymore. What was the point?

"I talked to Karyn Shelly today, Robert." Karyn Shelly was my accountant. "You know how much you're spending per day in this place?"

I stared at Charlie. What an interesting-looking fella. His face was bright pink from the sun. He had zero hair on his head. He almost always wore these little circular glasses like John Lennon. His mustache had apparently siphoned all of the hair from the top of his head and sprouted it down at lip-level. His mustache was so . . . vast. It looked very unfriendly to the touch, too, like the bristles of a push broom. He was talking but I wasn't really absorbing his words.

"An average of about twelve hundred bucks a day, Robert. Twelve hundred. Some days considerably more. One day you ordered three thousand dollars worth of caviar and champagne. Parking your car down there at the valet alone is costing you a small fortune. Are you even listening to me, Robert?"

"Charlie." He seemed surprised that I was responding to him.

"Okay? Yes?"

"You know . . . if you shaved your mustache, right now, you would have some seriously fucked-up tan lines on your face."

Unamused, he turned to leave.

"Hey, hey. Charlie. Wait."

He spun back around at the door. "You know, you're joking, but this isn't a joke. This is your life."

"I know, I know. Take it easy."

"No, Robert. I'm trying to help you. And you're mocking me. So no. I will not take it easy. You've been my client for a long time, Robert, but you know what? Truth is, I barely know you. So I don't have to take this abuse, Robert."

Please stop saying my name every two seconds.

"We aren't friends, Robert. You're a client. I'm doing

this because you seem to have no one else. Okay? So the very last thing I need is to take abuse from a drunken asshole who hasn't paid me and hasn't left his lavish hotel room in"—he checked his watch—"I don't know, thirty-some-odd days, and is quickly running out of money. Okay, Robert?"

I stared at him and thought about it. "Okay, Charlie."

"Okay, then," he said. "Can we talk seriously now?"

"Yes. Seriously, Charlie, if you shaved that thing I bet it would still look like you had a 'stache! Because of the sunburn!"

He muttered something under his breath and turned and left, slamming the door behind him.

"The skin underneath that monster hasn't seen daylight in years!" I yelled to the door.

I crashed my head back into my pillows, smiled to myself, and went back to sleep.

My phone rang a lot but I never answered it.

I was growing quite sure that the two little Mexican maids, Rufina and Esperanza, were up to no good.

Often I would lay in bed in a haze, staring at the shadows underneath my doorway. Most of the time the shadows would just walk on by. You know, guests or hotel workers in the hallway going about their business. But sometimes, *sometimes* they would stop. *Sometimes* they would stop, and just stand there. In front of my doorway. And they'd stay there for way too long. This started happening every single day. They never came *inside* anymore, at least not when I was awake. They hadn't cleaned my room in who knew how long. But I think they might have been stealing clothes from my luggage when I was asleep. I just couldn't get my head straight enough to remember what was in there, and what might be missing. And sometimes there would be trays full of empty plates, large meals that had been ordered to my room and eaten. But not by me.

The whole thing was questionable at best.

I made a mental note to myself that I should really do an inventory of the stuff in my luggage, and also come up with some better system of sneaking up on these bitches so I could catch them in the act.

Spy on me? I don't fucking think so!

Day 101 at the hotel.

I know this because when I woke at about eleven a.m., ready to start my watch on the Shadows Under the Door, someone had slipped a note underneath it.

A communiqué from my Mexican nemeses, perhaps?

I rolled out of bed and picked up the envelope from the foot of the door. The name "NATHAN VACARIO" was printed on the outside. *Who the fuck is Nathan Vacario?* I thought. I tore open the envelope and pulled out a neatly printed, two-page letter from within. It was printed on stationery that read across the top in very serious type: FROM THE DESK OF KARYN SHELLY, C.P.A. The body of the letter read:

Mr. Vacario,

I have done my best to reach you many times over the past months. I am at my wits' end. I'm hoping this letter finds you, because I am fresh out of ideas and patience. It is my job to inform you that you are very close to bankruptcy, Mr. Vacario. You have now been staying at the SHUTTERS ON THE BEACH hotel for exactly 100 nights. The total sum of your bill, which I have been paying on a weekly basis, is $128,111.14. According to my accounting, you have $8,313.53 left in your Bank of America checking account, which, to my knowledge, is your only bank account.

The bad news, Mr. Vacario, is that you owe your attorney, Charles Walter, $15,550 for services rendered during the divorce from your wife, Ava, and for his firm's services rendered in the Jordan Coulter suit. You owe me $3,848 for my services over the past three and a half months. After these payments, you will be negative $11,084.47.

I understand from Mr. Walter that you have a vehicle parked at the hotel that is fairly new and should fetch somewhere in the range of $40,000. Mr. Walter can arrange the sale of this vehicle for you. I recommend you call him and instruct him to do so immediately, to prevent any major problems.

Mr. Vacario, on a personal note, it is not my business, but I further recommend that you take the remaining money, check out of the hotel, and find yourself a decent, or even a mediocre place to live, before you spend every last penny you have. Charlie and I can help you do that.

Please contact myself or Charlie Walter AS SOON AS POSSIBLE to arrange for the sale of your vehicle.

I know you are going through a terrible time, but you can pull out of this, Mr. Vacario. It's not the end of the world, though I know it must feel like it.

Best,

Karyn Shelly

KARYN SHELLY, C.P.A.

I put the letter down. *Who in the FUCK is Nathan Vacario? Maybe Karyn is using a pseudonym for me, just to be safe? Just in case someone else found this letter? Clearly, the letter was meant for me. I don't get it.* I picked up my cell phone and powered it on. I looked up Charlie Walter's number and called him.

"Charles Walter," he answered.

"Hi, Charlie. This is Bobby Flopkowski."

"What can I do for you, Robert?" *All business.*

"I need you to sell my car, Charlie."

"So you spoke to Karyn. Yes, I can do that for you. That should be, uh, that shouldn't be a problem."

"Thank you, Charlie."

"No problem."

"Charlie, do you have any idea who Nathan Vacario is?"

There was a long pause, and then, "Are you okay, Robert?"

I chuckled. "We're not friends, Charlie. You work for me, remember? Please sell my car, take what I owe you plus whatever percentage you think is fair, and give the remainder to Karyn Shelly. Tell her to keep paying the bill here till there's nothin' left."

Charlie seemed to give that some thought. "*Robert,*" he said after exhaling deeply.

"Thank you, Charlie." I hung up.

I popped a large, oval-shaped pill, and surveyed the dwindling reserves.

Nathan Vacario. Nathan Vacario. Nathan Vacario.

It rang a bell somewhere in the depths of my foggy mind.

"Who is Nathan Vacario?" I asked the little blue teddy bear. And then I fell asleep. Wash. Rinse. Repeat.

CHAPTER
Twenty-one

One day when I woke up there was a mountain of new crap piled up in my room. A whole bunch of it, neatly stacked against a wall. I propped myself up onto my elbows and stared at the heap. I couldn't immediately identify what this junk was. There were boxes and bags and I spied a tennis racket and some ski poles and a red metal box that looked like an old tool kit. I sat all the way upright. The red metal box set off some alarms, some memory in the recesses of my mind struggling to breach the surface, but I couldn't get lucid enough to remember why. I ruffled my hair and wiped my face with both hands. My head began to clear some, aside from the click-clack-clicking.

This must be the stuff from my house that Ava put in the car. Charlie sold the car.

I dragged myself out of bed and swigged some rum. *Note to self: rum is an excellent morning drink.*

I made my way over to the pile of stuff. Surveyed the clutter. Worthless junk. Nothing I needed. *Maybe if I give it to the maids they'll stop spying on me.* On the outskirts of the mountains of crap, I spotted the tent and sleeping bag that Dicky had given to me for my birthday. It hadn't been all that long ago, but it seemed like ancient history.

I decided to open the tent and pitch it. I thought it might be fun to sleep in it, right there on the hotel room floor. Like being a kid again and building a fort. This would actually be the first time I'd be using it. Dicky and I never got to take that trip he'd planned. I had the inexplicable suspicion that the clicking sound in my head would not follow me into the tent. I pulled the canvas and the metal rods out of the sack and began assembling it. It took much longer than it should have. Mostly because I took several liquor breaks, and possibly a few quick naps. I'd flop down on the bed for what seemed like just a minute, but each time I'd wake to discover that hours had passed.

It was dark when I eventually finished constructing my little yellow bivouac. I unzipped the door flap and crawled inside. I was drowsy from all the hard work, and also because of the copious amounts of medication and alcohol pumping through my veins. Which reminded me: I jumped out of the tent and grabbed a bottle of Johnnie Walker and a handful of pills. En route back to the tent, I caught sight of that red metal toolbox, and it halted me. I glared at it, trying to remember its significance.

Only one way to find out.

The box was dusty and cobwebby and cold to the

touch. I unlocked the two latches, and slowly opened the lid . . .

Tools.

Nothing remarkable. There was a rusty old hammer, a screwdriver with a hard blue plastic handle, an adjustable wrench, a wire cutter, needle-nose pliers, a bunch of loose screws and nails and wire and assorted other detritus.

That was on the top shelf.

There was a handle with which to remove this upper section of the toolbox. I lifted it, and, underneath, found a small cloth bag with a drawstring on top. I removed the bag. It was heavy and familiar.

I instantly remembered what was inside.

I slowly opened the satchel.

I reached in and pulled out one of my father's antique handguns.

It was a Remington. A .45 caliber Colt from 1875. It had a beautiful wood handle and a very rare, shorter factory-correct 5 $^3/_4$ inch barrel. "Extreeeeemely rare, you understand? Extremely! Won't see this nowhere else!" Dad would say. He was so proud of this gun. He cleaned it relentlessly. "Still works!" he would always crow. "Long as you keep 'em clean, these suckers'll last forever. Just yer basic mechanics." He would take me out to Long Island to a field and we'd shoot at tin cans. Then we'd go home and he'd walk me through the steps to clean each of the guns we'd fired. Aside from his novel, this was the only thing he gave a shit about, and one of the only fun things I can ever remember doing with him.

This was the gun he killed himself with. The one he left to me in his will.

This discovery seemed significant. A sign. A message from on high. I picked up the gun and turned it over in my hands. It was clean and rust free, I guessed from being kept inside the bag. It was heavy and cold and beautiful, and it chilled me to the bone. I looked back inside the red toolbox. Inside were all the supplies I'd need to clean the gun.

And also, a box of bullets.

I sat on the bed and disassembled the gun. Even in my intoxicated, cloudy state I could do this by rote.

I cleaned all the parts, put it back together, and tested it. Spun the barrel around like my father used to do, and cocked the hammer. I pulled the trigger.

Click.

Long as you keep 'em clean, these suckers'll last forever.

I grabbed a few bullets from the box. My head began to CLICKCLICKCLICKCLICK.

I loaded one into the chamber. I spun the barrel.

Like my dad used to do.

CLICKCLACKCLICKCLACKCLICKCLACK. *How could I stop the hellish, ceaseless clicking?*

I looked at the blue teddy bear next to the bed. Breathed deep. I thought of Ava and Jack. Both gone. I thought of my father again.

I brought the gun up to my head.

My hand shook as I pressed the cold barrel into my temple.

DO IT DO IT DO IT DO IT

Fuck it, I thought. I pulled the trigger and the gun went CLICK. Not the imaginary clicking sound I was used to. This one was real.

I gulped.

Pull it again, you chickenshit.

I held it against my head and closed my eyes.

I was going to pull it again. I really was. Five more times. End this torture. But then a thought crept into my brain and slid right down into my trigger finger.

You want to go out like your father?

I lowered the gun and stared at it.

I took a long swig of whisky.

The tap dancers in my skull were on the attack, big-time.

Maybe my dad was onto something. Maybe he wasn't such a coward after all. And anyway, my situation is way worse than my father's ever was! He killed himself over a stupid book he couldn't finish!

The book.

I hadn't thought about his book for a very long time. *The Human Being,* it was called. *Stupid title.* Even though he left the only copy of the manuscript to me in his will (along with this gun), I'd never read it. After all, it was responsible for the death of my father. I never wanted to fuck with it. What if it somehow managed to creep into my brain and infect me like it infected him? Ava always said I should read it, find out why it drove him mad, but I could never bring myself to do it. So

I locked it away with his gun and tried to forget about both items.

I looked over at the toolbox where I'd found the gun.

I walked over to the opened box and looked down at it.

There it was. The manuscript. Ruffled and yellowed with time. Sitting at the bottom of the box, just underneath the gun-cleaning supplies and bullets, challenging me to take it out and have a look.

I slammed the cover closed on the toolbox and walked over to the nightstand, grabbed the little blue teddy bear, popped an OxyContin, grabbed my bottle of whisky off the bed, and climbed back into the tent. I lay on my back on the floor, and stared upward at the opaque yellow material steepled above me. Just as I'd hoped, the clicking sounds didn't follow me into my little yellow hideout. It smelled great in there, clean and sterile, like a new car. Or a new tent. "You don't ever hear about that—that new-tent smell," I said to the blue teddy bear. "Underrated." I put my gun and the bear down on the floor beside me. I reached my arm out of the door flap and grabbed for my sleeping bag, which was stuffed into a very small sack, as the tent had been. I yanked it out, and spread it out over the floor of my fort. I lay down again, this time atop my squishy down sleeping bag. I enjoyed the silence for a minute. *Not bad,* I thought. *I could get used to this.*

Oh, how used to it I would get.

The whole world was shaking.

Earthquake, I thought, grabbing uselessly at the ground beneath me.

I was still in my tent. It was hot. I was sweating.

The whole thing shook wildly, canvas and poles banging and quivering.

And then: *"¿Señorrrrrrrrrr? ¿Está usted adentro allí? Allooooo?"*

It was one of the maids, shaking my tent. Not an earthquake. I reached for my gun.

"What? What the fuck do you want, spy?" I answered.

"¿Señor, por qué es usted en una tienda?" she responded. I couldn't tell which one of the spies it was, or what she was saying, but I really didn't care. I just wanted to sleep.

"Please go away! Out! Out!" I tried to remember how to say that in Spanish but I couldn't. I thought about firing a warning shot but was shrewd enough to hold off.

"¡Cuatro días, señor! ¡Cuatro días usted ha estado en la tienda!"

I didn't know what she was trying to tell me, but I didn't like the sound of it. It was menacing.

"You better get the hell outta here! You don't wanna fuck with me, lady!" I shouted. I raised my gun up in front of my face, the way the police do when they are sneaking up on a suspect. I heard what sounded like dishes clanging together. And then it sounded like she placed something just outside of my tent. I gripped the handle of my gun, and listened.

She left. I heard the door close behind her, and I

thought I heard her mutter *"coco"* under her breath. Something like that.

I unzipped the tent door flap halfway and cautiously peeked outside, leading with the muzzle of the pistol. She had left a tray with several plates of food for me. *Interesting,* I thought. *What's your angle, lady?* I suddenly realized how hungry I was. *How long have I been sleeping in here?* I reached for a croissant from a breadbasket on the tray. But as I brought it to my lips, it dawned on me: *That shady bitch is trying to poison me!* I dropped the pastry, zipped up the tent, and thought, *Nice try, Mexico.*

CHAPTER
Twenty-two

Two pending disasters managed to come to fruition on the exact same day. I knew they would eventually come, and they came like a kick in the nuts. Hard and more painful than I thought they would be.

I'd been sleeping in the tent on the hotel room floor for several weeks. I didn't like to come out if I didn't have to. It was like a cocoon. The clicking kept out. I felt safe.

At least until I reached the very end of my pills. Kick in the nuts numero uno.

Somehow it snuck up on me. I didn't realize my supply was so low. I thought I had some more outside the tent somewhere, but I didn't.

When I realized I only had one pill left, an OxyContin, I maniacally rifled through all my stuff in search of some hidden stash that didn't exist. I tore apart my suitcases in a frenzy.

My heart pounded. My head CLICKCLICK-CLICKed.

I threw stuff around the room. I think I cried. Everything jumped and jangled like a poorly cut movie. I was wild. Unhinged.

I looked in the cracks between the bed and the headboard. I ripped the sheets off the bed.

There have to be some strays! I must have dropped SOMETHING!

I was completely freaking out.

I paced around, and then I took the last pill, just to calm the fuck down. I drank the rest of my last bottle of whisky and then shattered the bottle onto the bathroom floor. I ran to the phone to call down for some more.

The girl on the phone said, "Mr. Vacario? It says here you checked out this morning." Kick in the nuts, part deux.

My head began to swim. I placed the phone back in its cradle.

"Checked out"? "Vacario"? What the fuck is going on? Could my money be gone already? How long has it been since I spoke to Karyn? Since Charlie sold my car? I thought I'd have more time!

I started to shake. My heart slammed against my rib cage. I was sweating. The CLICKing in my head grew louder and more persistent. The tap dancers graduated to a machine gun.

How am I going to get more pills?

The phone rang.

I snatched it up without thinking.

"Hello?"

"Mr. Vacario?"

"Who the fuck is Mr. Vacario?" I spat, agitated.

"Mr. Vacario, this is Thomas Hess. I am one of the managers here at Shutters on the Beach. I just wanted to thank you for your extended stay here with us."

"Thank me? What do you want?" I asked.

"Well, Mr. Vacario, I received a phone call from your attorney, a Mister . . . Walter? Who tells me that you might need to be forcefully removed from the premises. Mr. Vacario, we *really* don't want it to come to tha—"

"Mr. Vacar—WHAT THE FUCK DO YOU WANT?"

"We want you to leave now, Mr. Vacario. Peacefully. It's eight p.m., and checkout was at three. We've been more than accommodating to you and your . . . peculiar behavior over the past months, and—"

"Your goddamned maids have been spying on me and stealing from me! You call *me* peculiar? I intend to file suit!"

"Mr. Vacario, I'm sorry that you believe th—"

I slammed down the phone. Ripped it from the jack and smashed it against the wall.

I looked around, frantic.

Why isn't this OxyContin kicking in?

I was sweating profusely.

CLICK-click-CLACK! Click click click!

I needed to get out of there.

I threw some clothes into my smaller, rolling suitcase. I took down the tent, but couldn't figure out how to get it into the sack. I folded the poles and shoved them into the sack. I slung the tent and my sleeping bag over my shoulder. It was heavy. I grabbed two plush white towels from the bathroom and threw them into my suitcase. I shoved my gun into the waistband of my pants, and a handful of bullets into my pocket. I grabbed the little blue teddy bear, gave it a kiss, and shoved it into my bag.

Near the door, just before I exited, I caught a glimpse of myself in the mirror above the desk. I hadn't looked in the mirror at all over the past few months. The sight froze me in my tracks. I was unrecognizable.

My eyes were sunken. My face was thin and sallow. My hair was wild and greasy and silver. I had a long, graying beard. I looked like I had aged a decade or more.

Truth is, I wasn't unrecognizable. I looked like my father at the end of his life. A lump formed in my throat.

I turned around and spotted the red toolbox on the floor. I walked over to it, opened the lid, and grabbed my father's manuscript from the bottom of the box. I looked at the cover. *The Human Being*. I decided to take it with me as a reminder that I didn't want to wind up like him. I shoved it into my bag and made for the door again.

I looked at myself in the mirror one more time. *You don't look like your father, you look like a homeless person!*

I left the hotel.

CHAPTER
Twenty-three

It was dark outside.

A chilly night, a cool wind off of the ocean.

Every light had that star-like, blurred quality. Every sound was louder than it should be, like someone had turned the sound all the way up on the world. The chattering of the palm fronds in the wind. The car horns. The buses. The engines, the people, the doors opening and closing. And of course, the clicking. I felt like a man walking on an alien planet. Like a stranger in a strange land. I hadn't been out in the world in . . . I wasn't sure how long. I didn't know what to do.

No money, no home, no car.

No Jack, no Ava.

No nothing.

All I had was the stuff I carried.

That's all I had left in the world.

I took out my cell phone and tested it. It still worked. For now. But who could I call? Charlie Walter? Karyn Shelly? Ava? Katie?

No. No. No. No.

Dicky.

I couldn't recall having spoken to him since that day in the office when I took a swing at him. Maybe he'd been to the house or the hotel to check on me? I couldn't remember. Maybe he'd spoken to Charlie Walter? I would think, after all we'd been through together, my best friend would care about my well-being enough to check up on me, even if he didn't want to be a part of my life anymore.

Also, Dicky might be able to give me some more pills.

I found his name in my phone address book and pressed SEND to call his cell phone. It rang a few times and went to voice mail. "This is Dr. Richard Sapp. Please leave a message." *Beeeep.*

"Dicky . . . it's me. Bobby. Call me, Dicky. I need you. I need help."

I hung up.

Now what? Where do I go?

It was too late to call Dicky at the office. I tried him at home. No dice. Answering machine. I left a message.

I was desperate for some alcohol.

I walked until I found a liquor store.

I tried to buy a handle of whisky.

I had four credit cards in my wallet. They all got rejected, one by one.

I asked if they had an ATM. They did.

I stumbled over to it, inserted my card.

I had no money in my checking account, but by some miracle, I had $47.98 in my savings account. I withdrew forty bucks and bought the whisky.

This will have to last me, I thought, looking at the large bottle and the life-giving amber liquid inside.

I walked outside, opened the bottle, and took a slug. I felt immediate relief.

I tried to call Dicky's cell phone again. Voice mail. I left another message.

My head was a blur, but I knew my priority was to get some meds in me, before I started withdrawing terribly. I could go down to the boardwalk and try to buy some pills off of someone. There had to be drug dealers down there.

I didn't like that idea. Not at all. I was scared, really. I knew it could be a very dangerous place at night. I could easily get robbed (of what little I had left), beaten, or arrested. That was a last resort.

There was only one place I knew that I could definitely get my hands on some pills: my former office.

I was a few miles away and my only option was to walk.

I shoved off, my suitcase in tow, my tent and sleeping bag over my shoulder. The clicking was there in my head, but every time it reared up, I shoved it back down with a few glugs of whisky. I saw small, dark critters, maybe rats or squirrels, skittering across my path. I could hear their sinister chattering. I heard the ominous calls of crows *caw-caw-caw*ing above me in the dark sky. I was paranoid and jittery and savage. I felt like the living dead.

The office was much farther than I'd anticipated. It seemed like I'd been walking forever and making very little progress.

I was exhausted.

I called Dicky again. Voice mail. I said, "Dicky. Please. Please answer your phone. I am on my way to the office. I need your help, Dicky. Please."

I walked and walked and walked.

I made it to the office. I tried Dicky again. Nothing. I climbed the front stairs, where just a few months ago, I'd sat and petted my little doggy friend, Bob Barker. *I wonder what happened to that little fella?*

At the top of the stairs, stuck to the wall next to the door, was a plaque which had once read my name, Dicky's name, and Tobias Stenzler's name. Now it read Dicky's name, Stenzler's name, and the name Richard Wiggs.

Replaced. Just like that. By another Dick.

I tried the door.

Locked.

I looked around. It had to be about midnight now, and there was no one out. I looked at the door. There were four small windows set inside the frame. If I broke one of them, I could reach inside and unlock the door. I opened my suitcase and took out one of the towels. I wrapped it around the crook of my elbow, looked around for witnesses, and when I saw none, struck the lower left windowpane with my wrapped appendage. The glass shattered. I glanced around again. Coast clear.

I reached in and twisted the dead bolt, and then the little nub within the doorknob. I was free to enter.

I went inside. Upon entering my old place of work, smelling the familiar smell, seeing all the same art on the walls, I felt a pang of . . . regret? Nostalgia? This part of my life was over, and it seemed irretrievably so. *Look at me. I'm breaking and entering to get drugs.*

What the hell am I doing?

I left my gear just inside the door, and made my way quickly toward the room in which the sample meds were kept. *There should be plenty of goodies in there.*

I found the room and opened the drug cabinet. There were boxes and boxes of drug samples sent to the office by drug companies trying to convince the doctors that their products were the way to go. Every doctor's office has a cabinet like this.

Except in this particular cabinet, all I could find were allergy meds, antibiotics, and various non-narcotics. All worthless.

"FUCK!" I said aloud, as I tossed boxes onto the floor.

And then, from behind me:

"Bobby?"

I spun around. It was Dicky. He was standing in the doorway. He looked tanned and fit and healthy and handsome. When he saw my face a look of horror passed across his face.

"Dicky."

"Oh my God, Bob."

"Oh my God what?"

"You look . . . I don't know. I almost didn't recognize you."

"Well, things have changed. What can I tell you?"

"What are you doing here, Bobby?"

"What do you *think* I'm doing here, Dicky?"

"I honestly haven't the faintest. Bobby, are you all right? You really don't look good."

"No, I'm not all right. How did you know I was here?"

"You called me, like, ten times. You told me you were coming here."

"Okay. So? Are you gonna help me or just gawk and tell me how terrible I look?"

"Help you with what, Bobby? What do you need me to do?"

"I need fucking drugs, Dicky!"

"Flop—"

"Stop it. Cut the shit. I need *drugs. Now.* Do you understand what I'm saying?"

"I understand what you are saying, Bobby, but we don't . . . I can't give you drugs."

"Are you fucking kidding me? You *can* and you *will,* Dick. Because it's your damn fault that I'm hooked on this shit and I'm about to lose my mind, and all this cabinet here contains is fucking Flintstones vitamins. Get me some goddamned Vicodin or Oxy or Xanax or *something.*"

Dicky looked stung. For a moment I thought he was going to relent, but then his expression hardened. "Bobby, this is a pediatrician's office. We don't have drugs like that here."

"I know you have a stash, Dicky. We always kept a stash."

"Not anymore."

We stared at each other. I knew he was lying.

"Dicky, if you don't produce me some goddamned drugs right now, this is going to get ugly."

Dicky looked stunned.

"What has *happened* to you?" he asked.

And then it occurred to me that there was a very easy way to tip the scales in my favor.

It was tucked securely into the waistband of my pants.

I pulled out the gun and pointed it at Dicky. He almost fell backward.

"Oh my G—Bobby!? What the hell are you doing?"

"Get me the meds, Dicky."

"Bobby, where did you—you're gonna shoot me, Flop? What the fuck?"

"Pills. Where are they?" I said, in my coldest tone.

"They're . . . they're . . . they're . . . ih-ih-in my office."

"Show me."

Dicky just stared at me.

"Fucking show me!"

Startled, he turned and led me quickly to his office. Once inside, he went to a closet and pulled out a plastic tub full of small cardboard boxes. He handed me the tub.

I got down on my knees and tore the top off of the large bin. I felt like a pirate who had just discovered a treasure chest. I found a bunch of Valium and Xanax samples, and a ton of assorted painkillers, including OxyContin, which was my favorite. All in all, I came away with a few hundred pills.

Mission accomplished.

"You shouldn't have done this, Bobby. It didn't have to be this way," Dicky said from behind me.

I took three Valium, and choked them down without water. "Do you have any alcohol?" I croaked.

Dicky hesitantly pointed to a large, ornate armoire next to his desk. I opened one of its doors. There was a tall, thin, very expensive bottle of tequila, and a short, squarish, very expensive bottle of scotch. I took them both out of the cabinet, placed them down on Dicky's large mahogany desk, and took a nice sample swig of each.

"If only Ava and Jack could see you now," Dicky said. I felt like someone had punched me in the spine. I stiffened.

I slowly turned to him. "What did you just say?"

"You heard me, Bobby."

I raised the gun and pointed it at his chest. He took a deep breath and looked down at the barrel.

"Say it again," I dared.

"You may be in a bad way, Bobby. You may be a lot of things you never were before." He was spitting this all out in rapid fire. "But you are not a killer. You're not gonna kill me, Bobby."

I clicked back the hammer.

Dicky gulped.

I had no intention of shooting him. But I was very upset by the blasphemous words he'd just uttered and I wanted to scare the shit out of him. I stared at Dicky. Dicky stared at the gun.

"Do you have any cash?"

"You're robbing me, too?"

"Let's consider it severance." I felt the Valium and liquor kicking in, big-time.

Dicky reached into his pocket and pulled out his wallet. He had one hundred twenty-three bucks in cash. I reached out and snatched it from Dicky's quivering hand.

I was suddenly so drowsy I could barely stand. I took a wobbly few steps away from him.

I turned back to him, the gun still aimed his way.

"Pleasure doing business with you again, Dick."

"Don't ever contact me again, Bob. You hear me? You're dead to me."

Like I said, I had no *intention* of shooting him.

I pulled the trigger.

CHAPTER

Twenty-four

Somehow, and I haven't the foggiest idea how, I awakened comfortably in my tent in a park in Brentwood, hidden behind a huge cluster of bushes and shrubbery. There was a giant jacaranda tree outside my tent that was raining purple flowers on my little abode.

Okay. My first night on the street—not so bad.

My suitcase was right there in the tent with me. My gun was right beside me. Jack's teddy bear was in my hand. My dad's manuscript was under my pillow.

I couldn't remember anything that had happened in Dicky's office after I pulled the trigger. I didn't know how I got here or how far away I was from the office.

I didn't . . . no. I couldn't have.

I couldn't imagine that I would *ever*, no matter how intoxicated I was, shoot my old friend Dicky. *I remember pulling the trigger, but I must've just fired into the air . . .*

right?! It certainly wasn't premeditated! I just reacted! I would never intentionally shoot anyone!

I started to panic.

I pushed two Xanax out of their little plastic-and-foil wrapper, and swallowed them with some tequila. That helped. I tried to piece the previous night together. It seemed like a dream. Like it never really happened. But here I was with a fresh supply of pills, so it must have happened. I had no recollection of coming to this park or setting up my tent. How could I have done that in my impaired state?

It didn't make sense.

Nothing made sense anymore. I could have sworn my tent was yellow before.

Now it was red.

I didn't feel safe there in Brentwood. It's a well-to-do community, and the laws and the cops there are much less liberal than they are in Santa Monica. They were liable to throw me in jail for being an eyesore in their cute little neighborhood. And if I really *had* shot Dicky, they'd be searching for me.

I decided to make my way back toward the beach.

I spent a few terrified days hiding out in my tent, petrified that the cops were hunting for me. Every siren, every flash of light, every voice made me jump. I was keyed up and medicating myself in a desperate way.

At some point my fear subsided, and I slowly ventured back out into the world. But things only got worse. I began to black out more and more.

I would wake up somewhere and have no earthly idea how I got there. One time I awoke naked on the beach, lying in the wet sand, waves kissing my feet. Thankfully, it was before the sun came up, so no one saw me.

One time I came to in a Dumpster, with rotted food all over me, stuck in my beard and on my clothes. I had a putrid, sour taste in my mouth like I'd been eating the garbage.

Once I was lying in an alley, my stuff piled neatly next to me. A homeless woman I'd never seen before, her head on my lap, reading my father's manuscript.

On a street corner at noon. Under some brush on the side of the freeway. In the stairwell of a large parking structure. On a bench at a bus stop in the middle of the night. On a grassy hill near some tennis courts. In a port-o-potty on the side of the Pacific Coast Highway.

One time I awoke in my tent with blood all over my hands.

Rock bottom? Not yet.

I'd been living on the street for what I calculated to be roughly twelve weeks.

I was inebriated to a dangerous point at all times.

I'd taken to chopping up my pills and snorting them up my nose. Fucked me up more. Sometimes I would buy or steal a bottle of cough syrup and drink the whole thing in one shot. Made me hallucinate and trip. That was always fun.

The clicking sounds in my head were driving me mad.

When I was somewhat lucid I would do my best to pitch my tent somewhere safe and just stay put. But the blackouts were coming fast and furious, and I almost never awakened in the same place that I went to sleep. This was the most unnerving feeling in the world, but I felt I had absolutely no control over it. I'd always find my tent and my stuff somewhere nearby, though sometimes I'd have to spend an entire day or two trying to find it. My life became a terrifying kaleidoscope of pills and booze and strange people and places.

I was circling the drain at a terrifying velocity.

Friday night in my twelfth week as a homeless man, things changed. At least I thought it was Friday night. I could usually tell by the exponential increase in the number of rowdy drunks going in and out of the bars.

I awakened on a sidewalk, leaning against a building. There were a lot of people walking by. Young people and couples, mostly. Some of them would glance at me with pity or disgust in their eyes, and not even break stride.

There was another homeless guy a few feet away from me. He had a black dog tied to his wrist. They were both sleeping. I felt sluggish from whatever drugs were in my system. I pulled a flask-sized bottle of cheap bourbon from my jacket pocket. I drank it until it was gone. I looked in my "drug compartment" on my little rolling suitcase. I was beginning to run low. There were about thirty or forty assorted pills in there, floating loose without bottles or identification. I reached in and took one. I couldn't tell which was which anymore. Didn't matter.

I looked around. I recognized the area. I was about

one hundred yards from Ava's favorite restaurant. The place we would go for her birthday every year, and for anniversaries, and whenever she needed cheering up after a bad day. Expensive joint, but the food was fantastic.

My mouth began to water. I was hungry. I decided to go check out the Dumpster. Maybe some skinny rich bitch didn't eat her lamb chops and they'd be waiting there for me with a side of mashed potatoes.

I was about to get up when a couple walked past, hand in hand, and something about them stopped me.

It was the woman. I recognized her walk, even from behind. But more than that, it was the hair. Her remarkable white blond hair swayed in a familiar way.

Ava.

I said her name aloud.

I thought she was too far away to have heard me, but she turned and looked at me. We locked eyes. She cocked her head and squinted.

Then she turned to her companion and said, "That homeless guy just said my name!"

"Oh, c'mon, hon. Don't be silly," he said. She snuggled up to him, like she needed protection from imminent attack. They laughed and he kissed her cheek. He reached past to open the restaurant door for her, and I got a good look at him.

Dicky.

Alive and well and apparently fucking my wife.

Rock bottom.

CHAPTER
Twenty-five

I felt the tears on my face and before I knew it, I was weeping.

"Whatsamatter, Vacario?" said the homeless guy lying next to me.

My bawling morphed into a bestial wailing, and then I began to scream. It was primal. I didn't care about the people looking at me. I screamed like someone had just ripped my guts out.

I tore open my suitcase compartment and scooped all of the pills up into my hand. I looked down at them in my palm. They were all different shapes and sizes and colors.

Should be enough to finish the job.

I found a bottle of whisky in my bag, thought about my father for the most fleeting moment, and then swallowed every last pill I had.

I didn't want to die there on the sidewalk. I decided to die on the beach, which was only about a block away.

I crossed the street to the bluffs above the Pacific Coast Highway before the drugs took effect.

Just a little farther to the place where the road sloped downward toward the Santa Monica Pier and the sand and the ocean and my final resting place. A sense of peace came over me.

As I slugged along, I glanced to my right and saw a man standing on the railing at the edge of the cliff. It appeared that he was about to jump. The cliff was very high and the rocks below were jagged and the man would surely die a painful death if he were to take the plunge.

I stopped and watched him sway on the precipice. I was drawn to him, so I changed course and walked over to the railing. I stood below and stared up at him. The man was African American. He was massive. All muscle. He wore a pair of tattered pants. He had no shoes, no socks, and no shirt. He had bruises and wounds all over his body.

"What are you doing?" I asked him.

He was startled by my presence. He glanced at me, but didn't answer.

"You gonna jump?" I asked.

He nodded his head solemnly.

"Why?" As if I were one to ask.

He turned and threw a hard glare at me. "I got *nothing*," he snarled.

I could see the reflection of wet tracks running down his face. He looked cold and beat up. He turned back to the cliff, and stared out at the dark ocean beyond.

I was getting drowsy. I looked down at my suitcase and my tent.

"There's a clickin' in my head like a thousand typewriters that won't go away," he said quietly. My eyes widened. "I can't handle it no more."

I unzipped my suitcase and pulled out a large hooded sweatshirt. "Here. You can have this. It will keep you warm." He didn't take it. "I don't need it anymore," I said.

He looked at my offering, but didn't say anything.

I placed the sweatshirt on a park bench next to me. "In fact, you can have all of this," I said. I unzipped my suitcase so he could see all the clothing inside. I had his attention now. He was checking out my bag. I spotted Jack's blue teddy bear. I took it out, gave it a kiss, and shoved it into the pocket of my pants. I closed the bag. "And here"—I held up the tent in its stuff sack—"a tent. A roof over your head. And a sleeping bag." I held that up, too. "The clicking sounds can't get to you in this tent."

He looked at me in disbelief. He pivoted on the wide railing so he was facing away from the cliff now. Watching me.

"I don't have any food. But I do have fourteen dollars in cash, so you can buy yourself something to eat." I put the cash on top of the sweatshirt on the bench.

I was so tired now. I didn't have much gas left in the tank. I was having trouble keeping my eyes open.

"Oh and one last thing." I pulled my father's gun out of my waistband, and showed it to him. "No one will bother you when you've got this. There are bullets in the suitcase," I slurred. "Take care of it. My father gave it to me." My father, who'd also taken his own life.

Here I come, Dad.

Fading fast, I reached into the bag and felt the manuscript in my hand. I felt a brief pang of regret that I'd never read it. I'd never find out what the fuck was so goddamned heavy about this book that forced him to such drastic measures. *I'll take it with me to the afterlife. Give it back to him and tell him thanks but no thanks.*

I looked back up at the black guy.

"Where did you come from? Who are you?" he asked.

I was swaying in place now. Having trouble staying on my feet.

I thought about his question.

"I don't know," I said. And then I collapsed.

CHAPTER

Twenty-six

When I first awoke in the hospital, on my second or third day there, the black guy was sitting in a chair against a far wall, looking at me from the shadows. My father's manuscript was open on his lap.

When he noticed that my eyes were open, he spoke. "I ended up jumping after all. We both dead. Welcome to heaven."

I looked around. This room looked achingly familiar but I wasn't sure why.

"Kidding," he said with a small smile. "We alive."

I managed a smile, too.

He rose and stepped out of the shadows. "I was done. If you hadn't appeared, like a angel sent from God, I'd be a pancake at the bottom of that cliff."

"Mmmmm . . . pancakes," I rasped.

My body felt like I'd been run over by a bulldozer.

I was sore everywhere. I was starving. But my brain was working. There were no clicking sounds in my head.

Despite the fact that I was in a hospital bed with all sorts of tubes and monitors attached to me, I felt strangely like a man reborn. Like someone had put fresh batteries in me. The weight I'd been carrying around on my shoulders had somehow been lifted.

"Yeah, doctor says you can't eat no solids for a while. Till your stomach gets back to normal."

"Bummer."

"Yeah, well. You saved my life, John. That's why I'm here. Breaking my cardinal rule."

"Your cardinal rule?"

"I don't ever leave the beach. That's why they call me 'Coastal Eddie.'"

"Why don't you ever leave the beach?"

He looked down at the floor. He clearly didn't want to discuss this.

"That's okay, Eddie. You don't have to tell—"

"My baby died there. My baby and my girl."

I didn't say anything.

"I ain't never told no one that before," he said. "But you saved my life."

"I lost my family, too, Eddie."

"Yeah?"

"Yeah. That's why I ended up here."

"Me, too, John," he said, and I knew we were bonded from then on.

I tried to stretch without pulling the IV out of my arm. "Why do you keep calling me John?"

"John Doe. That's what they call you here. You ain't got no ID so they don't know who you are."

"That'll be good when the bill comes," I said.

"Damn straight," said Eddie, with a smile.

"How long do I have to be here?" I asked.

"Don't know. I ain't a doctor."

"I am."

"Huh?"

"I'm a doctor. I was a doctor. Before I became . . . you know, homeless."

"Yeah? For real?"

"For real."

"Okay, Doc. That's cool. That's real cool."

"What are you reading there?" I asked, even though I knew.

"This is yours," he said.

"Yeah. My dad wrote it. Do me a favor. Don't read it."

"Oh shit . . . o-okay. I'm real sorry." He closed the manuscript and put it on the bed. "I didn't mean to, uh—"

A nurse entered, saving us from the awkwardness. "Well, well, well! Look who's awake!" She was fat in the face and her body was almost perfectly circular. Her chin and neck were one and the same. She had very rosy cheeks and thin, stringy hair. She looked like an apple with arms and legs.

"This is Maurine, your nurse," said Eddie. I knew her name was Maurine because it said so on her gold necklace, and on her name tag, and it was stitched into her scrubs in bright pink. It was also written on the dry-erase board by the door, with little hearts drawn all around it.

"And what might your name be, my friend? I'm getting pretty tired of calling you 'Johnny Doe!'"

This lady is gonna get annoying quickly, I thought.

"I, uh, I don't . . . I don't remember," I said, with a discreet wink to Eddie.

"No? Gosh," said Maurine. I couldn't tell if she believed me or not. "Well, you just rest up, okay? You've been through a whole heckuva lot. You were in real bad shape when we gotcha. I'm sure it'll all come back to you soon."

"Okay," I said meekly. Eddie smiled. The nurse didn't even acknowledge him. She was probably scared of him. He's a fearsome dude.

"How are you feeling today?" she asked me.

"How you think he feelin'?" Eddie asked in mock outrage.

"Like I got hit by a truck."

"Well, I sure hope someone got the license plate!" she quipped, and then cackled. I had to close my eyes to prevent her from seeing how aggressively I was rolling them. I looked at Eddie. He lifted his shirt slightly to show me my dad's gun in his waistband, and raised an inquisitive eyebrow. I laughed.

"Now, what is so darned funny?" asked Maurine.

"I'm just glad to be alive," I said.

And for some reason I couldn't quite grasp, I really meant it.

I spent twelve days in the hospital. They had to pump my stomach, and then I had to detox for over a week. My joy at being alive quickly faded.

Detox was agony.

Constant shaking and sweating and vomiting. I couldn't breathe and my whole body felt like it was being squeezed in a vise.

Eddie stayed with me the whole time. He very rarely left the room. Then, on my twelfth night there, when I was feeling up to it, he helped me sneak out of the hospital in the middle of the night. I'd managed to play the "I don't remember anything" game for the entire time I was there. They knew I was full of shit. I wasn't the first homeless guy who couldn't afford to pay the bill, but they couldn't move me until my condition changed from "critical."

Eddie asked me where I wanted to go, and I told him I wanted to go to the beach. I really didn't care where we went, but I knew he was dying to get back there, so that's what I said. I could tell he was silently grateful.

We made our way from the hospital to the beach, which was about seventeen blocks away. It was slow going. I hadn't used my legs in almost two weeks. I was sore and weak. We stopped at a mini-mart and bought a package of hot dogs and some Gatorades. It was almost dawn when we made it to the shore.

We pitched the tent on the sand.

I dove into the ocean.

This is my baptism, I thought, as I held my breath and felt the cold water envelop me. *Jack is gone. Ava is gone. Dicky is gone. Katie is gone. The drugs and alcohol are out of my system. The pain of detox is over. The paranoia. The clicking in my head. The anguish. Gone gone gone.*

I lifted my head out of the water. *I am a new man. This is my new life.*

Eddie and I cooked the hot dogs on sticks over a small fire. We watched the sun rise. We ate.

I felt like a human being for the first time since Jack had disappeared.

While we ate, I asked Eddie, "Do you know my real name?"

"Nope," he said, around a mouthful of hot dog. "You just 'Doc' to me, Doc."

"Good. That old name is dead."

"Okay, Doc."

"Will you help me, Eddie?"

"I'll do anything for you, Doc. I owe you."

"Just help me stay on the straight and narrow," I said. "That's all I ask."

"Shit, that's easy, Doc."

"I feel like I've hit the reset button. I think I can find a way to live again."

"You been through the worst of it, Doc. You just had to get through that darkest part of the forest before you could come back out into the light."

I stared out at the pinkish sky. The light.

I don't need anything that I needed before. I've been given a second chance. I am going to live without fear or worry or regret.

I am going to live.

CHAPTER

Twenty-seven

So we lived.

Eddie and I.

And we weren't alone. Not by any stretch. There was a whole community of homeless folks living in and around Santa Monica and Venice Beach, and we knew them all. And they all were characters through and through. They had great nicknames, or "street names," as the cops called them. Mine, of course, was "Doc"; Eddie, "Coastal Eddie." There was "L.A. Phil," a man who played a violin with no strings; "Sam Francisco," a flaming homosexual who always wore roller skates and skate-danced while carrying a boom box playing funk music; "Brick," a small, thick man who claimed to be indestructible, and was always running full speed into walls and trees in order to prove it; "Tampa Bay Ray," a guy who dressed like a pirate every single day and had a real live parrot on his shoulder named Achoo who was constantly making sneezing sounds.

But my favorite of all these characters was a little Hispanic guy named Manny Pedí. He was a sweet kid, in his twenties, a quiet loner who didn't talk much, but he liked to listen to us and laugh at our jokes. When you got him going he laughed like a hyena. He had long, dark, oily hair and acne-scarred skin. He had painted finger- and toenails. He looked up to me, and at some point, he started hanging with me and Eddie on a regular basis. He was just sort of there one day and he never left. The three of us became inseparable.

We lived on the beach.

We walked all day long. Up and down the coast, sometimes on extended excursions that would take us as long as weeks at a time and as far as the Mexican border.

We talked and talked and talked. We theorized about life. We laughed.

We ate mostly the leftover food we got from restaurants. Sometimes we ate at shelters. We never went hungry.

We kept ourselves very clean. Showered at the beach.

We slept in our tent. Sometimes we slept under the stars.

We got to know all the local cops. They liked us. We were the good guys.

We were nomads. Drifters. Vagabonds.

Free and unencumbered.

And we were happy.

CHAPTER
Twenty-eight

Five years passed like this.

My beard grew quite long. So did my hair. I was skinny but my muscles were taut and well defined.

I wasn't the soft and privileged wimp I'd once been. For the first time in my life I knew what it was like to be a real human being.

I was like a zoo animal, set free from years of captivity.

I'd managed to find real and true contentedness in this new life.

And then, at some point, things began to get a little weird again.

It started with the noises in my head.

I woke up one morning and there they were. Click. Click. Click.

I was horrified. I told Eddie about it. He said he heard them, too.

And then I started growing suspicious about Manny. It was nothing I could put my finger on. There was suddenly this dark, nebulous cloak that seemed to envelop him. He was up to something, I was sure, but I couldn't figure out what it was. His behavior was peculiar. Erratic. I would catch him stealing furtive glances at me. I began to suspect he was going through my stuff when I wasn't paying attention. I had the inexplicable feeling that he was after my father's manuscript. I started carrying it tucked under my belt, hidden under my shirt, instead of leaving it in the bag.

Also, and here's where it gets admittedly strange, I couldn't quite explain it and I didn't mention it to Eddie, but I could swear that Manny was somehow reading my thoughts.

Yep. Sounds even more preposterous on paper. It was just the way he looked at me. Like he was sucking information through some invisible mental bendy straw that was stuck into my cerebrum. When I was in moments of deep contemplation, or sometimes when I was sleeping, I would look over at him and he'd be *staring* at me, eyes squinted in intense concentration. And then he'd quickly look away.

And he knew things. Things I didn't remember ever speaking aloud. He would offhandedly make a comment about something from my past, some minutia or some random idea I'd been thinking about. It was bizarre and off-putting. I didn't trust him.

One night soon after I'd started worrying about Manny, we had a small fire on the beach. We'd just eaten dinner and I was taking a nap, snuggled up to the heat. Eddie wasn't around. When I woke up, I could see through the fire that Manny was reading my father's manuscript. I sat up and blinked a few times, just to make sure I was seeing it right. I was.

"Manny! What the hell are you doing?"

He slowly looked up at me, staring intently through the flames. He didn't look guilty or ashamed at getting caught. He looked . . . smug, for lack of a better term. Like he knew something that I didn't. And then his eyes did something strange. They went wide and began to glow. For a moment, through the scrim of the flames, he looked like some kind of demon, and I screamed and backpedaled away from him in the sand. "What the fuck!" I yelped.

Manny jumped up and walked toward me.

"I know the truth, Doc," he said in a calm voice, his head tilted slightly to one side.

"What's wrong with you, Manny?" I said, still backing slowly away from him, as he crept toward me.

"It is you who has something wrong."

"What?"

"The Devil is in you," he said in a throaty whisper.

A chill went up my spine.

"You've run for a long time. But he's back."

"Who's back? What are you saying, Manny?"

"Nothing is real."

The CLICKing was in my ears, loud and wild.

He opened his eyes really wide and I swear that his eyeballs glowed orange. "You will be tortured for your blunders. You will burn for your sins. You will die like your father."

I turned and ran away at full speed.

CHAPTER
Twenty-nine

I ran for what felt like a very long time. I didn't look back until I was quite far down the beach. When I finally stole a glance backward, I couldn't see Manny, but our fire looked much larger than it had up close.

A bit farther down the beach, I ran into Eddie. He was headed back toward our camp with a bag full of fast-food cheeseburgers.

"EDDIE!"

"Whoa, whoa! Whatsamatter, Doc?"

"Manny," I sputtered. I was out of breath from running on the sand.

"What happened to Manny? Is he okay?"

"He . . . he . . ." I tried to catch my breath.

"What the fuck, Doc? He need help?" Eddie dropped the bag of burgers and started to run toward our campsite.

"NO!" I shook my head and put my hands on my knees. Eddie stopped. "He went crazy, Eddie."

"What do you mean?"

"His eyes were glowing, Eddie. He said the devil was in me."

"*What?*"

"Scared the fuck out of me!"

"Well, let's go see what's up with him."

"NO!" I grabbed his arm. "Don't go back there, Eddie, I'm telling you. Something is not right with that guy."

"The fuck that li'l muhfucka gonna do to me?"

"Eddie. I'm telling you. This was . . . inhuman."

Eddie saw the fear in my eyes and began to believe what I was saying. "Okay, Doc," he said hesitantly. "I ain't never seen you scared like this. Let's just stay here for a while."

"Let's keep walking," I said. "I don't know if he followed me."

I didn't sleep that night. I sat on the beach with my knees up, my arms hugging them.

I didn't feel safe until the sun came up.

When it was fully light out, Eddie and I decided to walk back to our campsite to check things out.

It took us a while to trudge there in the deep sand.

When we got there, Manny was gone. The campfire was burned out, and in the pit were the charcoaled remains of all of our stuff.

Our tent.

Sleeping bags.

My suitcase.

All of our clothes.

Charred.

Instinctively, my hand went down to my pocket, just to make sure that Jack's little blue bear was still with me. It was.

Something on the ground caught my eye. I looked down to see my father's manuscript sitting there in the cold sand, safe and unharmed, the curled, bound pages flapping in the breeze.

CHAPTER
Thirty

A few days after the Manny incident, Eddie and I were still dazed and mentally wounded, but trying to recover.

We couldn't wrap our minds around what had happened. It was so sudden and senseless. I mean, I'd had a feeling that something was up with Manny, but what made him flip on us like that?

Why did he burn all of our stuff? Why did he leave my father's book?

My mind reeled and my pulse quickened every time I thought about what Manny had said.

The Devil is in you. You've run for a long time. But he's back.

CHAPTER
Thirty-one

S o here we are again. Full circle.

Eddie and I watched the sun rise and I trudged my way up to the Pacific Palisades to have breakfast at Café Emily with my friend Cecilia.

"What a nutcase!" she said. "Why would he burn all of your belongings?"

"I have no idea. He just . . . *turned* on us."

"I think my husband *might* have a tent," she said. "I'll ask him. He certainly never goes camping, so if he does have one, I'll just give it to you."

"Oh, Cecilia, that would be incredibly generous of you . . ."

And that was when it happened.

An SUV pulled up to the curb across the street and parallel parked. It was a dark gray Range Rover. Expensive. Typical in this part of town. I watched over Cecilia's shoulder as the female driver finished parking, shut the engine off, and exited the vehicle. She looked pretty from afar, though I couldn't yet see her face. She was tall and skinny and athletic, and she appeared to be heading to a yoga class. She pulled a rolled purple mat out of the backseat of her car and stuck it under her arm. She wore tight, expensive-looking workout clothes. She had a large leather purse slung over one shoulder. She reeked of money. She had a head full of beautiful wavy, caramel-colored hair. She turned and crossed the street in our direction. I did a double-take. Stopped talking, midsentence. Dropped my fork.

It was Katie Turner.

CHAPTER
Thirty-two

"What's wrong, Doc?" I heard Cecilia ask.

"I know her," I croaked.

"Oh yeah? Me, too."

Katie disappeared into a building a few doors down from the café, and I looked at Cecilia after finally registering what she'd just said. "What did you say?"

"I said, 'Me, too.' Her name's Kerri. She comes in here all the time."

"No, no. That was Katie Turner. That woman's name is Katie Turner."

"Nope. Trust me, Doc. Her name is Kerri. Kerri Taylor. She eats here all the time with her son. Goes to that yoga class almost every day. Lives around the corner on Lynar Street. She's married to some guy in a band or something, I think."

"No, no, no." I stood up.

"Doc?"

"I'm sorry, Cecilia. Thank you so much for breakfast. I've gotta go."

I walked quickly over to the yoga studio. It was up a flight of white wooden stairs. I debated for a moment, and then decided to go up. When I got to the top, I tried to peer through the windows, but there were large white wooden shutters blocking my view, and I couldn't see inside. I knew I'd look like a real creepy weirdo if I tried to peek in the cracks, or if I went inside to check out the women, so I decided to wait downstairs for her to come out.

I waited at the bottom of the stairs for what must have been about forty-five minutes, when I turned and caught sight of myself in a store window. I was so skinny. My beard and hair were so long. My clothes were kind of dirty now, since thanks to Manny, I only had this one set, and I hadn't had the chance to wash them in the past few days. Would Katie even recognize me? And what did I plan on saying to her? After all, look at us now! We were so different than we were the last time we saw each other. I started feeling anxious. I stood there wringing my hands.

Women began exiting the class and walking down the stairs.

And I chickened out.

I turned and walked away as quickly as I could, before Katie would spot me.

I stopped a few hundred yards away and turned around.

There she was. Katie fucking Turner. It was her— there was absolutely no question about it.

I was awestruck by her beauty. Even after a workout, she practically glowed. Time and money had done wonders for her. I watched her gracefully make her way down the stairs and across the street to her SUV. She threw her stuff in the backseat, got in the driver's seat, closed the door, started the engine, and drove away.

I smiled. Katie fucking Turner.

CHAPTER
Thirty-three

The next day I met Cecilia again at the café.

"You sure left in a hurry yesterday," she said.

"There was something I needed to check out," I told her.

"Something called Kerri Taylor, hot chick in yoga clothes?"

I smiled, but then looked her in the eyes and told her seriously, "That's not her real name." Cecilia stared back at me, trying to figure me out, a "Whatchu talkin' 'bout, Willis?" look on her face. "I'm serious. I knew her very well before I . . . you know, in my last life."

"I gotta hear this," she said. "Tell me the whole story, Doc."

So I told her.

I told her about Katie and I growing up together. I told her the odd story about how we reconnected over the Internet, and about our lunch at Mr Chow. I told her about Katie's problems and how I'd offered for her to move in to our house and about the strain it put on my marriage. I told her about the kiss the night Jack disappeared, and how Katie left when everyone else left. I told her about how my guilt over that kiss and what happened during it led me to lose everything I ever had.

Cecilia listened. And when I was finished, she was holding my hands on the table and she looked like she might cry.

"What are you going to do?" she asked.

"I don't know," I said. "I mean, I want to approach her. I *have to,* right? We have such a history, and considering how I helped her when she was at her low point . . ."

"And she lives on one of the nicest streets in the Palisades, and you don't even have a roof over your head—"

"Well, yeah, I guess there's that."

"You should do it, Doc."

"Yeah?"

"Yeah. If it really is her, she owes you one! But can I make a suggestion?"

"Of course."

"And you won't take offense?"

"Never."

"Maybe clean yourself up a bit before you approach her. You know, a shower, fresh set of clothes. Not that you're dirty—"

"No, I understand. Completely."

"Okay, good. Can I bring you something nice to wear?"

"No, that's okay, Cecilia. You do enough for me already."

"I insist! I love makeovers!"

Cecilia was too sweet, and I couldn't say no. She promised to bring me something "snazzy" to wear the next day.

I wasn't so sure I'd be ready to make contact by tomorrow.

I spent much of the night thinking about how this could possibly be one of my last times sleeping on the beach. *Katie could be my ticket back to a better life. I could stay at her place a few weeks, get a job, save some cash, and get a small place of my own. This feels right. Like destiny.* I knew what I needed to do.

In the morning I trekked down to the showers bright and early and took a long cold one. I washed my hair and scrubbed myself shiny. I debated shaving my beard but decided against it. It was an important and symbolic part of me, like a comfort blanket. A badge of honor.

Eddie wished me luck and I hiked up to the Palisades to Cecilia's little café. She was just opening up for the day. She invited me in and told me I looked clean and ready, and to grab a seat while she cooked me some breakfast.

"Oh!" she shouted from behind a clanging of pans. "Here!" She handed me a paper shopping bag filled with clothing. "You should be able to find some decent duds in there."

I looked through the bag. It held several assorted

pairs of pants, about five different button-down shirts, socks, a belt, even a brand-new package of underwear that she must have bought for me at the drugstore. It was strange. No one had taken care of me like that in a very long time. I got a little choked up.

She looked at me, and without skipping a beat, said, "Oh stop. It's *so* not a big deal! Go try some stuff on!"

I went back into the bathroom and tried on a pair of khakis and a nice pink dress shirt from Banana Republic. Pink wasn't my color, but I wasn't about to complain. Everything fit great.

"Whoa-ho-ho!" Cecilia said when I came out. "Look at this stud muffin!"

"I *feel* like a stud muffin," I said.

"You look *ready*," she said.

"Good. I am ready."

Liar.

CHAPTER
Thirty-four

The plan was simple: Katie goes to her yoga class. When she comes out, I make my approach.

I sat in the café and waited. It felt weird and stalky. She eventually pulled up out front, just a few parking spaces away from where she'd parked the last time I'd seen her. Same routine. She got out of the car wearing a very tight and sexy exercise outfit, grabbed her yoga mat from the backseat, and with an expensive bottle of water sticking out of her expensive purse, she made her way across the street.

My heart pounded. The clicking in my head was growing louder by the minute.

Why are you so nervous? I thought. *She's your oldest friend.*

The one hour she was in class felt like six. Cecilia brought me coffee and rubbed my back. The coffee was only making me more jittery. When the clock said she'd be out in ten minutes, I decided to go wait outside. The café was more full than before and Cecilia was busy, so she just smiled, winked, and mouthed the words "Good luck" when she saw me get up.

I waited nervously at the bottom of the staircase, my head filled with the click click clicking. I stared at my reflection in the same window I'd stared at the previous day. I looked much cleaner now, but still so much different than the last time Katie had seen me. What would she think?

CLICK click CLACK! Click click click click.

I decided to move away from the door a bit. I didn't want to be right on top of her when she came out. I wanted it to look like we'd stumbled upon each other, not like I was watching and waiting like some kind of creep. I took a few steps away, turned around, and there she was! Coming down the stairs! The clicking hit a fever pitch. CLICKCLICKCLICKCLICKCLICK!

Katie was chatting with another woman from her class.

They were smiling and Katie gave a toothy laugh.

I took a deep breath.

CLICKCLICKCLICKCLICKCLICKCLICKCLICK CLICKCLICKCLICK

"Katie!" She'd just said good-bye to her friend and she was fast-walking across the street. Her head flinched slightly but she didn't turn around.

I called out again.

No response.

I jogged a bit, just to catch up. The clicking drowned out all other sounds. "Excuse me, Katie?" I tried one more time. This time she turned, but probably only because I was so close. She opened her car door and stood half behind it as she turned to me, like a shield between us.

"Sorry? Me?" she asked. The clicking stopped.

Up close she was even more stunning than I remembered. I felt like I got the wind knocked out of me.

It took me a second to recover and say, "Yeah, Katie. Hi." I smiled. She didn't.

"H-hello. My name isn't . . . Katie . . . sir," she said delicately.

I laughed and looked at her in the eyes. "Katie. It's me. Bobbo."

She looked bewildered and uncomfortable. Her eyebrows performed a little dance routine for me.

"I'm sorry. Have we met?"

She was very discreetly inching her way into the car.

"No, Katie. It's . . . I don't look the same. I'm thinner, and the beard, but look closely at my face. It's me! Bobby! Flopkowski!" I smiled my biggest smile.

Now she just looked remorseful.

"I'm so sorry, sir. But I don't recognize you. And I've really got to run. But I hope you have a great day, okay?"

She closed the car door.

I stood there next to her car, looking like a fool, as she started the engine and drove away.

CHAPTER

Thirty-five

What.
The.

Fuck.

I stood on the street with my hands in the pockets of my borrowed khakis, and I turned toward Cecilia's café. She stood there, out in front, watching me, with a sad expression on her face. She waved me over and gave me a hug when I got there.

"Didn't go well, huh?"

"No."

"She didn't want to help?"

"She pretended she didn't know who I was!" I said into Cecilia's hair. *Why would she do that?* I was dumbfounded. *Man, she pretended well, too.*

Cecilia pulled back from our embrace. "Are you serious?"

"Not even a spark of recognition," I said sadly, at a complete loss to explain what had just happened.

Cecilia was pensive. I knew what she was thinking.

"I swear it's her, Cecilia. I'm 110 percent positive. Believe me."

"Why would she do that? How could someone be so . . ."

"Callous?" I asked.

"I was gonna say 'cunty,' but yeah."

"I don't know. I don't get it. I just don't get it."

I looked down at the sidewalk and kicked a pebble.

"C'mon, I'll give you some pie. Pie always helps."

I didn't want to be rude, but I wasn't in the mood. "I'm just gonna go back to the beach. I need to lie down and think about this for a while."

— — — — — —

"You sure she recognized you?" Eddie asked.

We were sitting on the beach.

"Even if she didn't at first, I told her my name. She certainly knows my name," I responded, throwing a handful of sand toward the water. "I realize I *look* different than I did five or six years ago, but I'm still me, right? I mean, the essence is still there. Under the beard and the sun-damaged skin . . ."

"You're still Nathan Vacario."

I whipped my head toward Eddie.

"What did you just say?"

Eddie smiled.

"That's your real name, right? Vacario? Somethin' like that?"

"No. That's *not* my real name. Where did you get that from?"

Eddie's smile vanished. "I'm sorry, Doc. I didn't mean to upset you. It's just . . . we been like family for so long, and you ain't never told me your real name. You always just been 'Doc' to me. But I heard you say that name a bunch a times in your sleep."

"In my sleep?" My head was clicking again. I was disturbed by this line of conversation. It was making me sweaty and uncomfortable.

"Yeah, Doc. Like, all the time. You always sayin' that one name. So I thought . . ."

"My real name is Dr. Robert Flopkowski, Eddie."

"Aight, Doc. No problem."

I lay back on the sand and looked up at the sky, at the clouds.

"That life is over," I said.

But that life wasn't quite over yet.

CHAPTER
Thirty-six

I couldn't stop thinking about Katie Turner.

I obsessed over it. For days and days. It was all I thought about. I kept going back to that interaction on the street. I replayed the conversation in my mind. I saw the expression on her face. I just couldn't reconcile what had happened. It didn't make sense! Katie had no reason to play it the way she played it. Why pretend she didn't know me? If she didn't want to help me, fine. *That* I could at least wrap my brain around. People are weird about money, and five years could certainly change a person. *After all, look at me.* She'd changed in the opposite direction. I wondered how she'd gotten so wealthy. Maybe she married rich.

But why pretend to not know who I am? Maybe she was just so thrown off by the sight of me that she just . . . *reacted?*

If that was acting then give the lady an Oscar.

And an earlier revelation now acquired new intrigue: *Why had Katie changed her name?* Was that connected to her performance on the street?

I thought about almost nothing else but this for days. I decided I needed to do a little further research.

With the clicking in my head and the crows circling in the sky far above me, I went back to the Palisades.

This time I didn't go to Café Emily, but to the library instead. They had computers there that the public could use, free of charge. I wanted to see if I could figure out how to find Katie's street and maybe also her exact address.

I typed the name "Katie Turner" into Google. A ton of results, but nothing to do with the Katie Turner that I was looking for. I tried "Kerri Taylor." That got a few relevant hits. The first one was a link to something called "Facebook," which I had never heard of. It said "Kerri Taylor—Los Angeles, CA." I clicked on it, and it took me to a page that said, "This is the public search listing for Kerri Taylor." It had a few tiny pictures of several different people, with a caption over the pictures that said, "Here are some of Kerri Taylor's friends." And then, right next to those, a slightly larger (but still pretty small) picture of "Kerri." Below her picture it said, "Kerri Taylor is a fan of: Music: Victor Taylor." Out of curiosity I clicked on the name "Victor Taylor," which took me to a new page.

My heart skipped a beat when this new page loaded.

I looked at the face of "Victor Taylor."

It was Katie Turner's boyfriend, Vincent.

- - - - - -

Not that there was any doubt in my mind before, but this cemented it.

No question. No doubt. 100 percent fact. It was Katie.

Katie Turner, Kerri Taylor. Vincent, Victor.

So they changed their names but kept their initials. Tough code to crack, folks.

So this is how they made their money. It appeared Vincent had some measure of success as a musician, after all. I read his "fan page," and found out that he was the guitarist for a band called Courtesy Flush. Lame. Never heard of them. Further searching told me that Courtesy Flush was a one-hit-wonder band who had a number one hit in 2003 called "The Color of Awesome." Barf.

I searched around online for a few minutes, trying to find a home address, but I quickly realized it wasn't going to happen.

I went to Google Maps and typed in "Lynar Street, Pacific Palisades, CA." A little arrow popped up on a map of the Palisades, directing me right to it. Luckily for me, it was a pretty short block, and not very far away. *Around the corner,* as Cecilia had said the other day. I figured out how to get there from the library, and headed in that direction without much of a plan.

I didn't want to confront her again. Not yet at least. I was thinking of this as a sort of reconnaissance mission. I would observe. Take notes. See what I could figure out by watching from afar, before deciding if I wanted to give another go at communication.

I stopped in to see Cecilia en route, since it had been a few days since we last chatted.

"There you are! I was getting worried!" she said when I walked into the café.

"No need to worry," I said.

"I'm sorry she treated you that way, honey. Just forget about her. We'll spit in her food next time she eats here." She winked at me.

"Ah, I wish I could forget it. I can't stop thinking about it, though." I told her what I'd discovered about "Victor."

"Rich people are weirdos, Doc. Narcissistic, egomaniacal weirdos. You gotta just say, *'C'est la vie.'*"

I looked down and shook my head. "I can't."

She lifted my chin up with her hand. "What do you mean, you can't? What are you gonna do?"

"I gotta talk to her again. Find out what the deal is."

She shook her head. "Doc, you better be *really* careful how you do this. People are . . . sensitive in this town. Especially if this guy is even a quasi celebrity. They get handled with kid gloves. If you mess with them—"

"I'm not gonna *mess* with them, Cecilia, I just want to talk to her. She's one of my oldest friends, I just want to . . . I don't know. I don't know *what* I want. I'm gonna go find her house and figure it out from there."

She was still shaking her head. She gulped. "Doc, maybe you shouldn't go to her house."

"Cecilia, I promise I'm not going to do anything that could get me in trouble. I'm just gonna look around."

"Just be careful, okay? This makes me nervous. If she feels threatened, you could get arrested or something, and I really don't want to see that happen."

I found Lynar Street without difficulty, and strolled down the block, trying to look like an average guy out for a walk. No one bothered me or looked at me funny. The cross street was Sunset Boulevard, a few blocks southeast of the little village where Cecilia's café was. Lynar Street only ran a few hundred yards long. There were only five houses on the block, two on one side, two on the other, and one at the end of the cul-de-sac.

The houses were quite large, but not mega-mansions. They all had extravagant, lush landscaping, and lots of arugula in the refrigerator, I was sure. *This is what my house might've looked like if my life had taken a different path. Me and Ava and Jack.*

It was the first time I'd thought about them in a while, and it put a little lump in my throat.

I wondered where Ava was and how she was doing. I wondered if she was still dating or maybe even married to Dicky. Maybe they had children together. The thought didn't upset me like it had before; rather, it comforted me. I hoped that Dicky—though he was a pussy-hound in his younger days—would be a committed and trust-worthy husband and father. Maybe he hadn't been so committed to *me*, but my memories of those times were shaky at best, and I knew deep down that I'd been the one to burn that bridge beyond repair.

I wondered if Ava thought about me. If she forgave me. If she knew what my life had become in her absence. I sincerely just wanted her to be happy.

I strolled down the street and looked at every house I

passed. *Might as well call this block Easy Street. These people have got it made.*

When I got to the end of the block, I spotted Katie's Range Rover tucked comfortably in the open garage of the house at the very end of the cul-de-sac.

Speaking of easy . . .

CHAPTER
Thirty-seven

I spotted a FOR SALE sign on the sidewalk in front of the house next door to Katie's. The front gate was unlocked, maybe so Realtors could get in to show the house to potential buyers. I quickly went inside the gates and scoped out the house. It was empty. No furniture inside.

I found a discreet spot on the side of the house on a wooden bench that was blocked from the street by rows of shrubbery, but gave me a pretty good line of sight to the entire front of Katie's house. I could sit there and see their door, their garage, and most of their front lawn. Perfect.

I don't know exactly what I hoped to discover, but I needed to see her again. I needed to know more about the mysterious "Kerri Taylor," because something wasn't right. Strange things were afoot. I needed answers.

I sat there for several hours. It got dark out. The lights went on inside Katie's house, and on the brick walkway up to their front door. But I didn't see anything more. I debated sleeping there, but decided it was too risky. I walked the ten or so blocks back to the beach.

I turned it over and over and over in my mind. I remembered that I'd tried to reach out to her several years back, but her phone number and email address had both been changed. *Curiouser and curiouser.* The more I thought about it the more crazed it made me.

What kind of person would do this? After I'd opened my home to her? After she witnessed the greatest tragedy of my life?

"Only a seriously crazy, cold-blooded *bitch* does some shit like that," Eddie said, as if reading my mind. "Unless . . ."

I looked at him. "Unless what?"

"I mean, what if it wasn't just a spur-of-the-moment brush-off? Maybe she'd prepared for that moment beforehand."

"Like, she knew I was coming?"

"Yeah. Maybe not at that exact time, but yeah, maybe she knew you'd come eventually. Or she at least had a plan in case you ever did come."

I thought about that, but it didn't quite make sense to me.

"How would she know I was coming? And why would she have to prepare for it?"

"I don't know. But if she really is Katie Turner, and

she *was* lying or acting or whatever when she saw you, then she *must've* been prepared beforehand. And if she was that well prepared, she must have a damn good reason."

Eddie might have been onto something.

Maybe she'd heard that I was homeless now, and she figured that when I found out how rich she was now, I'd come looking for a handout that she didn't want to give.

Seemed like a stretch.

It's gotta be something more than that.

— — — — — —

I went back to Katie's house the following afternoon. I felt a little bit uncomfortable walking down the block this time. I had the sense that I was being watched. I made a mental note to wear a hat or something to alter my appearance the next time I came. I was thinking that if I had a dog with me I'd look much less conspicuous. Something about walking a dog makes you look totally harmless. Where was my old friend Bob Barker when I needed him?

I walked up to the gate of the house next door to Katie's as confidently as I could, very careful not to look around or do anything that would reveal that I didn't belong there. I strolled right in and resumed my post on the bench.

It didn't appear that anyone was home at Katie's house. I sat there for several hours, twiddling my thumbs, before there was any activity.

Just before sunset, Katie's Range Rover pulled in to the driveway, followed closely by some kind of very expensive-looking silver Mercedes sports car. Katie got out of the Rover, and Vincent, aka "Victor," got out of the Mercedes. He looked, from afar anyway, the same as he had five or six years ago when I'd last seen him. Long black hair, sunglasses even though it was getting dark, black tank top, tats covering his arms, leather pants, black boots.

Katie opened the back door of the Rover and unlatched her child's safety belt. The kid immediately jumped out of the car and ran into his dad's arms. Victor picked him up in the air over his head. I could hear the kid giggling.

How wonderful for them.

I looked back to Katie. She was looking at the street, her head slowly panning from one side of the street to the other. They went inside, and that was all I saw for the night.

CHAPTER
Thirty-eight

The next day, I was walking through the Palisades Village to Cecilia's café when I spotted Victor's car parked at a meter on the street. I instinctively ducked into the nearest doorway. I peeked out, looked both ways, and when I determined that the coast was clear, I moseyed on over to the parking meter. It showed that he had nine minutes left before he had to put more money in.

Perfect.

I went back to my doorway. I came up with an easy way to test the guy. But first I'd have to wait.

Nine minutes passed with no sign of Victor.

Ten minutes. Eleven minutes. Fifteen. Nothing.

I was about to give up and go to Cecilia's when I spotted the creep strolling down the sidewalk to his car and his expired meter with absolutely no urgency. *What's a measly parking ticket to a rock star?*

It was go time. My plan didn't require even stepping out of the doorway. I only needed to be able to see him, from a location where he could not see me. The deep doorway provided such cover. Time to see if he could pass the test that Katie had almost failed.

When Victor got to his car, to the spot where I could see him but he could not see me, I shouted, "Hey, Vincent!"

The schmuck turned his head and looked.

Gotcha, fucko.

Unfortunately, my plan didn't end up the way I'd hoped. Victor did some further investigation and walked over in my direction. My heart began to beat faster.

Oh shit oh shit oh shit.

He spotted me standing there in the shadows of the doorway.

"Did you just say something to me?" he asked.

I kept my head down, tried to ignore him.

"Hey! You! Did you just say something to me?"

I looked up at him. We stared at each other for a minute. I could have sworn I saw some deep recognition in his eyes. Even the faintest trace of a smile in the corners of his mouth.

"I thought you were someone else," I said.

His eyes narrowed. He looked me up and down. When he got back up to my eyes, he tried to look real tough. He took another menacing step toward me, and in a quiet growl, snarled, "You stay away from us."

Then he turned and walked away.

CHAPTER

Thirty-nine

"H e threatened you?" Cecilia asked.

"He said, 'You stay away from us.'"

"I told you, Doc. You gotta be careful. They're gonna call the cops on you!"

"No, Cecilia, you don't get it! He responded to the name Vincent! Doesn't that prove that they are who I say they are?"

"I don't know, Doc. The names Victor and Vincent sound pretty similar."

"Yeah, but why did he tell me to stay away from them? Why would he say it that way if he didn't know who I was? If he thought I was just some crazy homeless guy or something wouldn't he have just said 'Stay away from *me*'? I don't know . . . it just seems like that was an odd choice of words."

"Maybe his wife told him about you approaching her the other day and he put two and two together."

"I don't know about that. Seems far-fetched that she would tell him that story if it didn't have some greater significance to her. It wasn't like we had some major run-in. I didn't harass her or anything. And even if she did tell him, I have a hard time buying that he would know that I was the same person who approached his wife just by looking at me."

"The alternative seems way more far-fetched to me. Sorry, Doc."

I looked out the window, let out an exasperated breath. Cecilia looked very troubled.

"Doc, I really think you should try to just forget about all this. Nothing good can come of it."

It was clear that she didn't believe me. I was feeling anxious and the clicks were CLICK-CLICK-CLICKing. I took a deep breath and tried to play it cool.

"Yeah. You're probably right," I said.

She looked at me with sympathy in her eyes. "Hey, guess what?"

She jumped up and disappeared into her office at the rear of the café. She came out holding a bright blue stuff sack, and in her best game-show-host voice said, "A new-wwww tent!"

"Oh, that is so great, Cecilia! Thank you so much! It's going to be nice to have a roof over my head again."

"I'm so glad. You'll get much better use out of it than my lazy husband."

"I think I'll go down to the beach and show Eddie our

new home!" I said enthusiastically, though I had no intention of doing any such thing.

I went back to my spot on the bench at the house next door to Katie and Vincent's. After my run-in with Vincent-cum-Victor, I was scared shitless that they would spot me as I walked down the street, but I made it there without incident. They didn't appear to be home. It was about three p.m.

At about four p.m. the front door opened and Katie came out with her son. The little boy had a soccer ball in his hands, and he ran to the lawn and tossed it down. He was wearing a blue soccer jersey, which was too long for him, and matching shorts. He dribbled the ball around in a wide circle on the grass. Katie watched and clapped for him.

"Go Joshua!" I heard her say.

Joshua.

He was a cute kid, at least from afar. He had a shock of very blond, almost white hair. A wheatish color that reminded me of Ava's. He turned in my direction and gave the ball a mighty kick and it sailed toward me. I flinched and then smiled to myself when I realized that Katie couldn't see me because of the tall hedges that lined the chainlink fence. Joshua ran over to retrieve his ball, and I got another glance at him. There was something about him that made my heart feel like it was being squeezed in a vise. He turned away from me before I could get a good long look at him.

I rose to my feet and leaned in closer, trying to get a

better angle through all of the bushes on the other side of the fence. Joshua was focused intently on his soccer ball, dribbling around in circles, this time on a swath of grass closer to where I sat. When he turned to face me again I got my first real, long look at him, and the whole world slammed on the brakes.

CHAPTER

Forty

J ack?" I whispered.

What is happening What is happening What is happening

As I watched the boy, the whole universe quaked. It was like watching footage of myself at this age. As he concentrated on the soccer ball, his mouth hung slightly open, his jaw cocked to the side the very same way I recalled doing as a kid. And he looked so much like Ava it was astounding. I simply could not make sense of what I was seeing.

That is my son!

Suddenly, he was standing there, right in front of me. Right at the gate. The ball practically at my feet. He was staring at me. He blinked in the most innocent way. He cocked his head slightly. I smiled in complete awe.

The song I used to sing to him, "You Are So Beautiful," popped into my head.

"Who are *you*?" he asked. Even the voice sounded like a chipmunk version of my own voice.

"I . . ." I realized that I had no idea what to say to the boy.

My son. Stolen from me so long ago. And here he was. Towheaded and precious and safe. But he had no idea in the world that I even existed. What could I say that wouldn't scare him? What could I do so that he wouldn't alert his mother to my presence? I glanced up and saw that Katie was pacing around the brick path which led to her front door, talking on her cell phone. She wasn't watching. I knelt down to the boy's level. I stared at Jack. He was the most beautiful child I had ever seen.

"I'm . . ."

"Joshy! What are you doing back there, hon?" Katie called.

I put my finger to my lips and said, "Shhhh . . . ," and I smiled in the most childlike, conspiratorial way I could. My boy smiled back. The tears welled in my eyes.

"Coming, Mom!" he said. And he was gone.

I was paralyzed.

I wanted to stand up and do something. Anything. But I could not. JACK! My son! Alive! *How how how how how?*

What now? I couldn't leave. What if he came back? I needed to see him again. I needed to stare at him. I needed to hug him and smell his hair and tell him that his dad was here now and that everything would go back to normal.

This is *his normal.*

It hit me like a gunshot in the gut.

He doesn't know who you are.

I fell to the ground on my ass, dazed.

I brought my knees to my face and I cried.

It had gotten dark, and I wouldn't be able to see him again tonight. I needed to think this whole thing out. How was this possible and what was I going to do about it? I put my hands to my ears to try to quiet the clicking, try to calm the deafening roar of the blood rushing through me, but it didn't help. I slowly rose to my feet. I needed to talk this out with Eddie. I left the house in a daze, and walked back to the beach.

Eddie had a fire going. I was still crying when I got there. I simply could not stop.

"Doc? You okay? You crying? What happened?"

I shook my head. I couldn't speak.

"What happened, Doc?"

"J-Jack," I sputtered.

I was uncomfortable in my own skin. I felt like there were bugs crawling on me.

I felt feral and out of control, like an escaped animal.

Eddie had his hands on my shoulders now, he was leaning down to my level and looking me in the face. "Jack? Your boy?"

I nodded. "I saw him, Eddie. I saw him."

"What you mean you saw him?"

"He's alive. I saw him."

"What?!"

I looked him in the eyes, hard and serious. "I saw him, Eddie. Katie and her husband. They have him."

He escorted me over to the fire and we sat down. I told him what I'd just witnessed.

"How is that possible, Doc?"

I'd thought about it on my walk down to the beach.

"It makes sense, Eddie! She was there when he disappeared! It must have been a setup. They planned the whole thing!"

Eddie wasn't getting it.

"When we reconnected, it was no accident. She'd lost her own baby and she desperately wanted another one! They must've been watching me before she even contacted me. She knew she could get close to me. That night . . . she came inside the house with me and kissed me, just to keep me busy! And while we were doing that her piece of shit boyfriend stole my son!"

I pictured that scumbag creeping into my backyard and snatching Jack from his bassinet. Then I flashed back to Katie and me sitting on the deck, right before we went inside and kissed. Right before Jack vanished. *I wish there could be a happy ending for everyone,* she'd said.

"Fuck," Eddie whispered.

"She called him 'Joshua.' But it was my son, Eddie. There's no doubt in my mind. That little boy was Jack."

"Yeah, but, Doc, don't you think they would have gone farther away? Like, moved to another city or country or something? Changed their appearance?"

"I don't know! I admit it doesn't make complete sense, but none of it does!"

"What you gonna do, Doc?"

"I don't know. What *can* I do? Who is gonna believe me? Look at me and look at them! If I go to the police I'll be laughed out of the building or probably thrown in a cell or a psych ward!"

"Let's just go get him, then! Take back what's yours. We can run just like she ran."

I shook my head. "We can't. We can't do that. What would I do with him now? I don't have a home. No money. I couldn't take him out of that life, away from who he thinks are his parents, and force him into a life like this, on the streets."

"Maybe he remembers you, Doc."

"He was barely one year old when they took him from us, Eddie. There's no way." I thought about the way Jack had looked at me earlier through the fence. How he'd smiled. How he'd trusted me. There was a connection there for sure. *Maybe some small part of him* did *remember.*

"We gotta do somethin', Doc. They can't get away with kidnapping your kid. I don't care *who* they are!"

I thought about what Eddie was saying.

How can I possibly hope to change this situation?

And then it hit me. Ava.

CHAPTER
Forty-one

I woke up the next morning with fire in my belly.

The good kind.

I made a big, bold, brave decision to track down Ava and Dicky.

I needed them on my side. There was no way I could do this alone. I needed to tell them everything that was happening. After all, child or no child, they were the only ones I knew who could corroborate that Kerri Taylor was really Katie Turner. If I could *at least* get them to validate that part of the story, then maybe . . .

I would cross that bridge when I came to it.

First I needed to figure out how to find them—where they lived now. I thought about going to Dicky's office and confronting him there, but the last time I went to that office things didn't end so well.

I wondered if they might live in Dicky's old place. It

was a large apartment overlooking the water on Ocean Avenue in Santa Monica. I couldn't envision them living in an apartment. A house would be more likely. *Could they be living in my old house?* Doubtful, after all the bad shit that happened there.

I decided to check it out, just in case.

I took a bus to Beverly Hills. It took about an hour. My stomach tightened up as I approached the driveway, and my heart started to thud. Not so much because I was nervous to see Ava and Dicky (I really didn't expect that they would still be living here) but because I had so much history with this place. So much good and so much bad.

The house looked pretty much the same. The hedges had grown substantially higher. The trees, taller. The driveway was repaved. That was about it. The paint was the same color. It looked like maybe a fresh coat had been applied recently.

I stopped at the foot of the driveway and took a deep breath. I walked straight up to the front door and rang the bell. I stood there for a few moments, tapping my foot. Then I heard the old familiar clop-clop-clop of shoes on the wood floor of the foyer. The door swung open, and there was Ava.

We stared at each other for a moment, taking each other in. She looked stunning. Older, of course, but still as beautiful as I remembered. Her hair was the same ivory hue. Long and healthy. Her eyes the same impossibly bright blue. Those eyes examined my face. My beard. My own eyes. Then her head cocked ever so slightly to the side, as she registered just who it was she was looking at.

"Hello, Ava," I said.

And then she fainted.

She actually fainted! And she hit the floor *hard*.

I leaped forward to try to help her.

An approaching voice from the other room said, "Hon?"

And before I knew it I was being tackled to the ground.

I wrestled around for a minute with this unseen assailant, and then I ended up on my back with Dicky awkwardly straddling me, fist cocked back, ready to pummel my face. For a moment I thought he recognized me and would withhold the blow, but then his fist *slammed* into my mouth and I tasted blood as one of my front teeth pierced my bottom lip and my head banged hard against the floor. I managed to spit out something that sounded somewhat like his name before the second punch landed, and he paused, midstrike.

He stared at my face.

"Oh my God . . . Bobby?" he asked, slowly dismounting from me, and rising to his feet.

"Hi, Dicky," I said, through my split, bloody lips.

"What . . . is going *on*?" Dicky asked.

Ava had come to, and they were both looking at me now.

I looked at Ava. "We need to talk," I said.

We sat in my old living room, me on the big brown leather easy chair, the two of them on the green suede couch. The whole thing was completely surreal. I'd purchased all of this furniture years prior, and now I felt like I didn't have any right to be sitting on it.

The two of them could not take their eyes off of me. Nor could they keep the looks of—what was it, exactly . . . revulsion? Loathing? Fear?—from breaching the surface of their expressions. *How and where to begin?* ("Long time no see" didn't feel quite right.)

"Sorry about your lip," Dicky said, breaking our silence.

"It's okay," I said. "You didn't know it was me."

"No, I sure didn't."

"And anyway, last time I saw you . . ." I made a finger gun and a clicking noise as I pulled the imaginary trigger. No one laughed.

"Well, luckily you missed," said Dicky. "And you weren't in your right mind, so . . . forget it. Long time ago."

But it was obvious he was uncomfortable. *How could he not be?!* He didn't look the same, Dicky. My old friend and partner. Gone was the dashing, strapping young bachelor. He was a puffy version of his younger self. His black hair had gone salt-and-pepper. He was wrinkled and tired. He looked like a doctor now. A worn old doctor—finally—instead of a handsome young lothario.

Not that I was one to talk in the looks-have-changed department.

We sat in silence, none of us knowing quite what to say. What could we say? Where to begin?

"I'm sorry," I said. "For, you know, *everything.*"

"Don't," Ava said feebly, briefly making eye contact, before looking at something on the coffee table.

More uncomfortable silence.

"We visited you, you know," Dicky said. "After . . . well, when you were in the hospital for all that time."

"The hospital?" I asked.

"Yeah. The . . . hospital," he said. They glanced at each other for a moment, both looking uneasy.

I didn't know exactly when or what Dicky was talking about, so I said, "I'm sorry. I don't remember. Everything was pretty . . . blurry . . . for a while."

I wished I could recall their visits, but I was deeply grateful to hear that they hadn't abandoned me the way I'd thought everyone had.

He nodded. "That's okay. We know. You were"—they traded glances again—"not yourself."

I looked over at Ava. She looked completely rattled. She didn't know where to put her eyes. The floor? The couch? The coffee table? The ceiling? Anywhere but on me—her old, skinny, bearded, homeless ex-husband. The man who lost her child and sent both of our lives tumbling. I wanted to reach out and comfort her. Tell her that I still loved her and that everything might end up all right after all.

"Ava," I said.

"Why are you here?" she said with a start, staring hard into my eyes.

It wasn't an attack. Not at first. It wasn't said in a cruel or vicious way. It was an honest question. She didn't trust me. Shit, she didn't even *know* me anymore, nor I her.

Maybe this quiet, sort of gloomy woman sitting across from me was the new Ava. I had no way of knowing how Ava functioned now in her everyday life. If she was back to the joyful Ava I'd known before our lives fell apart. If she'd managed to move on from our loss, rebuild some semblance of a happy life with Dicky. Or if that event had fundamentally altered her the way it had me. What was clear was that my presence was stirring up a lot of emotions and she needed to know why I was forcing it upon her now.

"This isn't easy," I started off, looking down into my lap. "I know you are uncomfortable, Ava, and I apologize. I am uncomfortable, too. But I have something I need to tell you. And I wouldn't have come here if it wasn't very, very serious."

"You need money?" Dicky asked.

In my gut I badly wanted to hurt him at that moment. As if I would have gone there for something so trivial. I choked back my anger. "No. This isn't about money."

"So what is it? What would make you show up here like this after all this time?" Ava asked bitterly, the vitriol peeking out of its hiding place.

"It's Jack."

There. I said it.

I expected it to land with a little more impact, a little more *oomph,* but they both seemed unfazed. They glanced at each other quizzically and then back at me.

"What about him?" Dicky asked.

"He's alive."

Oomph now? Check.

But not the good kind of *oomph*. Ava let out a frustrated sigh and Dicky slapped a hand down on the couch and made an *uchhhh* sound. "Okay. I hoped it wasn't going to be something like this, but obviously you—"

"I'm serious!" I interrupted. "This isn't a joke!"

"I know it's not a joke. But c'mon, Bobby! What are you doing?" Dicky asked, rising to his feet.

"No! You have to listen to me! I saw him! With Katie Turner!"

"I knew this was a bad idea. I thought maybe you were . . . I don't know, *healed*. Don't you know somewhere in your head that this is a bad idea, Bobby? Can't you just let sleeping dogs lie?" he asked.

"*Listen* to me. I saw Katie Turner. She lives in the Pacific Palisades under the name Kerri Taylor. She is still with the scumbag guy she was with when she stayed with us! When Jack disappeared! *They took him!*"

I pleaded with them to listen. Ava just stared down at the coffee table, unmoving and unemotional, like she'd checked out of the conversation. Obviously Dicky didn't believe me, but I thought Ava might be taking it in.

"This is ridiculous, Bobby. You should go," Dicky said firmly.

"No! Please! Listen! Ava, they have a child! The kid is too old, I mean, the timeline, it . . . it doesn't make sense!"

Dicky moved over in my direction and gently grabbed my arm and tried to tug me to my feet to escort me out. I was desperate to finish.

"C'mon. Up. Let's go," he said.

"Please," I said. "They couldn't have a child that old

when she wasn't even pregnant when she lived with us! I mean—I, I know it sounds crazy but please! You have to belie—"

"Stop it!" Ava shouted.

I shut up. Dicky and I both froze in place.

"Just stop it. I can't listen to this!" she said.

"Please, Ava," I muttered gently, trying to connect with the woman I loved, who loved me back so long ago.

"No! You are not a sane person, Bobby. This is not *real*!"

"Ava, it's real. I swear it's real. His hair. He has the same exact hair as you and—"

"No! Please! GET OUT! You are crazy!"

"Ava," Dicky said.

"Shut up, Dicky," she spat. "I am not going to listen to this! I've spent enough time torturing myself! You lost your mind a long time ago, Bobby. We've seen you, walking the streets in Santa Monica, babbling to yourself."

"No," I said.

Babbling to myself?

"You lost your mind when you lost our child and you know what? You *deserve* it."

"No," I said softly, barely able to speak with the proverbial knife in my gut. I looked at Dicky, who was looking down at the floor now, ashamed. "I'm not crazy," I said in a whisper.

"Yes, you are. You lost it, Bobby. Just like your father." *Ouch.* "And I won't let you sit here and dredge up all of this terrible baggage that I've spent all of this time trying to dispose of. It's not fair."

"Ava—"

"Please get out," she said resolutely.

I swallowed hard, trying to hold back the tears, and then got up and bolted. Dicky followed behind me, and once we were out of the living room, out of earshot of Ava, Dicky, still on my heels, said, "Let me give you some money, Bobby."

But I was already gone.

CHAPTER
Forty-two

It was a difficult night. I was wounded badly by Ava's rejection and by her harsh words. Somehow, after agonizing over it for a while with Eddie, I managed to banish it to the far reaches of my brain. After all, there was only one way to substantiate everything I had said to her.

I went back to Katie's house the next day. I had to see him again. I had to confirm my belief and find a way to prove it to Ava and Dicky.

It was Saturday. I got to the house very early, around seven a.m. It was quiet for a while. They were late sleepers, I supposed. At around nine a.m. a maid walked outside to get the newspaper from the foot of the driveway. I imagined that she would go back inside and cook an elaborate breakfast for Mom and Dad and my kid. Pancakes, eggs, bacon and sausage, orange juice, coffee. The works. My mouth watered.

They stole what could have been my life.

At about ten a.m. the front door opened and two kids bolted outside. The first kid was Jack. I didn't recognize the other kid, but figured that it was a friend of his, and that they'd had a sleepover. Katie came out a minute later to watch over them. They asked her to open the garage door and get them the soccer ball.

A few minutes into their play, Jack chased the ball in my direction, and I got my first good look of the day.

My heart soared at the sight of his face. As if he felt the intensity of my stare, he stopped and looked over at me. I don't think he could see me, but it was as if he'd just remembered that I'd been over there the day before last. He stood there for a minute and stared.

"C'mon, kick it!" his friend shouted, breaking Jack from his reverie. Jack spun around and kicked the ball to his friend, but before running back over to where his buddy was, he turned once more and quickly glanced toward me. I smiled.

Katie chatted away on her cell phone. This time she sat on the front steps, leaning back on one elbow, casually talking and watching the kids.

Less than a minute later, I watched Jack very purposefully kick the ball in my direction. He kicked it much harder than necessary, and directly at me.

"What are you doing?" his friend whined.

"Stay here and we can kick it alllll the way back and forth across the wholllle lawn."

I knew right away what my smart little guy was doing. He ran to the ball, which had stopped about twenty feet away from me on the grass. He gave it one more good kick and it flew over the bushes and hit the gate right in front of me. I stood up. And there he was.

He popped out of the brush like some kind of elf from another world. His skin pristine porcelain, his hair a feathery white puff. He smiled when he saw me.

"Hi!" he said.

"Hey!" I responded quietly.

I knew I only had a few moments with him. I wanted to make them count. I reached into my pocket and felt Jack's little blue teddy bear. I pulled it out. It looked a little dirtier and more tattered than I'd hoped, but I was relieved that I had it with me.

"This belongs to you," I said.

"Me?" he asked.

"Yup. It's yours. From a long time ago. I held on to it for you."

"It's mine?"

"Sure is," I said.

It was hard to talk to Jack without bursting into tears or grabbing him and running. But I didn't want to scare him.

"I can keep it?" he asked hopefully.

I nodded. "It belongs to you. And look at this," I said. I pulled the sleeve of my shirt up on my left arm to show him my tattoo of the bear and his name, but when I pulled the fabric high enough up on my arm to reveal it, the tattoo was gone. I was bewildered for a moment, but then the bushes rustled and the other little boy popped out of them. He was even smaller and skinnier than Jack and he had curly red hair. He stopped dead in his tracks, wide-eyed, when he spotted me. Jack looked busted.

"Who're *you?*" the other kid said.

"I'm—"

"Joshy?" Katie called from afar.

"Gotta go!" said Jack with a grin. His little blue teddy bear in his hand, he took off into the brush, his friend in tow.

"What do you keep *doing* back there, Josh?" I heard Katie ask.

My heart dropped. I took a couple of steps backward.

"Nothinnnng!" Jack said in a whiny, leave-me-alone voice.

A pause, and then: "Josh, what is that? Come over here."

"Nooo!" Jack whined.

"Joshua Matthew Taylor you get over here *right now,*" she ordered.

I peeked through the bushes and watched Jack march over to Katie, the bear hanging from his hand.

"What is that?" she asked.

He begrudgingly handed her the dirty old stuffed animal.

"What is this? Where did you get this?" Katie asked.

"It's mine!"

"It's dirty and gross! Where did you find this?" she said.

I watched with my heart in my throat.

"It's mine from a long time ago!" he said.

My heart ached.

"I don't remember this thing. You just found it in the bushes?"

Jack didn't answer. He looked guilty.

His friend chimed in: "No! That man gave it to him!" He pointed to where I stood.

"What man?" Katie asked.

"The man hiding over there in the bushes!"

Katie stood up and looked in my direction.

I turned and ran.

CHAPTER
Forty-three

I ran as fast as I could around the back of the house and jumped over a fence. I ended up in someone else's backyard on the adjacent street. It didn't appear that anyone was home at this house. At least, they weren't in the backyard or close enough to any of the back windows that I could see them. I got out of the yard and onto the street as quickly as I could.

I jogged away. I was going to head to the beach, but when I thought I heard police sirens, I decided to stop in at Cecilia's. I knew her serene demeanor would calm me down.

When I got there, wild-eyed and manic, Cecilia greeted me in her usual warm way.

"Well, if it isn't the Doctor himself! Where have you been, friend?"

I realized that she didn't know anything about the newest twist in the story—the part about Jack.

"Doc, what's wrong? You look awful!"

I looked Cecilia in the eyes. She was so sincere and kind. There was so much compassion behind those eyes. I realized at that moment that she was the only non-homeless person I knew at that point. If anyone was going to help me, it had to be her.

"Come, sit," she said.

She pulled me over to a table. I put my head in my hands and began to cry. I felt completely unstable.

Cecilia didn't say anything, she just reached over and held my arm, rubbing it with her thumb.

When I pulled it together a bit, I said, "They took my son from me."

"Who took your son?" she said gently.

I exhaled loudly. I was scared to speak their names. I was afraid she wouldn't believe me. I knew how outrageous the whole thing sounded. I couldn't do it. I shook my head.

"Go ahead," she said.

I carefully told her what had happened. She already knew the part of the story in which Katie came back into my life. She'd already doubted that Katie and Kerri and Vincent and Victor could be the same people. Now I wanted to convince her that Jack and Joshua were one and the same. It was a losing proposition.

When I finished, Cecilia looked at me with a new expression. This one was pure pity. I knew I hadn't sold her.

"Cecilia, you don't understand, she actually said to

me, 'I wish there could be a happy ending for everyone,' right before Jack disappeared! Don't you see?!"

She reached out for both of my hands, and continued to look in my eyes. She was preparing to say something she did not want to say. "Doc, I care about you. You know that, right?" I didn't answer and she didn't wait for one. "I'm concerned about you. Can you talk to me straight? I want to ask you something and I don't want you to get upset."

I looked up at her. She continued, "Can you tell me . . . if you have a history of mental illness?"

"Oh, goddammit!" I stood up quickly, throwing her hands off of mine and knocking my chair over behind me. "I knew you wouldn't believe me!"

"Doc, please! I've watched you over the last week go from a very calm, carefree fellow to a complete maniac! You're crazy over this whole thing!"

"I'm not crazy!" *Why does everyone keep calling me that?!*

"I don't mean to say *you* are crazy, I'm just saying you are behaving in a way that does not seem . . ."

"Sane?"

She made a frustrated sound. "Of sound mind."

Tears filled my eyes again. My thoughts were frenzied and unmanageable. "Cecilia, you can believe me or not. You can choose to think I'm just some homeless nutcase. I don't give a shit. I am telling you that that boy is my *son*. I realize it doesn't sound rational but that is the God's honest truth."

"Can you prove it somehow?" she asked, desperately grasping for some way to believe me.

"Prove it?" I asked.

"Did your baby have any identifying marks or anything like that?"

"No. No, he was just a normal baby."

She exhaled exasperatedly.

"You gotta believe me, Cecilia. I know my own child when I see him!"

She looked down into her lap and slowly shook her head. "No," she whispered. "I'm sorry, Doc. I'm sorry. It's just not possible. It doesn't make sense. I'm sorry."

I stared at her.

She looked at me and then leaned over to emphasize what she was about to say.

"And I don't want you to do anything rash or dangerous," she added.

I turned and left without another word. I heard Cecilia say my name as the door closed behind me.

CHAPTER
Forty-four

I was heading back to the beach. I was walking along a white stucco wall in an alley, agitated and on edge, when I heard a far-off *CRACK,* and the stucco next to my head exploded in a sudden burst of stone and dust. I hit the ground, disoriented.

Someone was shooting at me! Another whoosh-*CRACK* and then the concrete by my leg erupted.

I jumped and yelped and managed to scramble behind a Dumpster.

WHAT THE FUCK WHAT THE FUCK WHAT THE FUCK?

My knees and hands were scraped and bloody from the pavement. I put my back to the green steel Dumpster, and tried to catch my breath and collect my thoughts. I heard another few *CRACKS* and then the Dumpster went PING! PING!

Holy shit! Who the fuck is firing at me? Vincent?

I crouched and counted to three and took off as fast as I could away from the Dumpster, trying to keep it between me and the shooter. I heard another *CRACK*. I made it to the end of the alley without getting hit. I looked around, trying to decide where to run and hide. There was a Starbucks about two hundred yards away.

I dashed for it.

I tore the door open and ran through the shop to the bathroom in back. I went in and slammed the door behind me. I locked it. I sat on the floor and closed my eyes and rocked back and forth and waited.

I waited for five minutes.

Ten minutes.

Twenty.

A knock on the door.

I didn't respond. Another knock.

I was sweating and holding my breath.

"Thir? Are you all right in there?" a voice asked.

I didn't dare respond. *You can't trick me, fucker.*

"Thir, if you don't come out we are gonna have to call the copth."

I debated this for a minute. Had I done anything wrong? And anyway, why weren't the cops here already? Gunshots in the Pacific Palisades? Why wasn't I hearing tons of sirens outside? What the hell?

"Go ahead! Call the cops!" I finally shouted.

I heard a grunt from the other side of the door.

I waited. Ten more minutes. Twenty. Nothing.

I decided to venture a peek out of the bathroom. After all, no one would be dumb enough to cap me right in the middle of a Starbucks, right? I opened the door slightly and peered out.

Coast clear.

I inched my way out of the room.

"About friggin' time!" said a lispy, pimple-faced Asian girl wearing a green apron. "I gueth you mithed the thign that thays *employeeth only?!*"

I looked around the shop. There were a few patrons in there, but no one even looked at me.

Maybe the sniper didn't see where I went.

Phew.

I cautiously left the Starbucks and ran ran ran back to the beach. I didn't leave my tent for the rest of the day.

CHAPTER
Forty-five

I had horrific nightmares that night.

There were massive, black, screeching beasts lunging at me from the sky, their razor talons glistening in the moonlight as they tried to snatch my baby from my arms.

When I woke up I was sweating. I decided to step out of the tent for some air. It was still dark, probably about four a.m. I felt like I was still dreaming. I could see inky shapes circling the sky above me, and hear unidentifiable noises all around. There appeared to be human-sized silhouettes walking out of the ocean, slowly, toward me.

Eddie wasn't there.

Where the fuck is he? It's the middle of the night.

We'd been talking when I went to sleep. He held the strong conviction that I had no choice but to go and get my boy back, and he made sure I knew it.

"Eddie?" I called.

No answer.

The beach can be a creepy place at night, and make no mistake about it: I was scared. I called Eddie's name again, but when I got no response, I decided to bolt.

I left the beach and headed instinctively up to the Palisades. I was deep in thought as I trudged my way up there. Before I knew it, I was at the foot of Lynar Street.

I took my post on the bench outside the house next door to the bastards that kidnapped my child. I sat there and stared at the house, tapping my foot and rocking a bit. *Jack is inside that house right now. My son. The reason my life fell apart is because those people stole him from me. He is alive. He is only a few hundred yards away from where I sit. He is mine. My flesh and blood. MINE. I must go get him. I must. I must. I must. It is my duty as a father to protect my child at all costs. I failed once. I cannot fail again. He is MY child. I must go get him. I must I must I must.*

I thought about Manny telling me that I would "be tortured for my blunders" and that I would "burn for my sins." I closed my eyes tightly and shook my head, as if I could will the thoughts out of my brain.

I looked up, and I saw a shadowy figure pass through a sliver of moonlight on the side of the house. At first I thought it was a figment of my wild imagination, like the frightening shapes I'd seen on the beach.

But then I saw it again, a few seconds later, a few feet away from where it had previously been. The shadow stalked slowly up to a ground-floor window and stopped, its back flat against the side of the house.

In the light of the moon, I caught a glimpse of the shadow's face.

Eddie.

- - - - - -

Fuck.

"Eddie!" I whisper-yelled.

He couldn't hear me. I was too far away from him.

I watched him duck under the window and disappear around the corner, to the back of the house.

Shit. Fuck. Shit. What do I do? What is Eddie going to do? I can't let him do something stupid! Shit! Fuck! Shit! Clickclickclickclickclickclick . . .

I didn't have a choice. I scaled the metal gate that stood between the two properties, and landed with a soft *thunk* in the dirt on the other side. I ducked and looked around to make sure I hadn't caused any disturbance loud enough to draw attention. All seemed quiet. I ran around the perimeter of the property, doing my best to stay behind the cover of bushes and hedges wherever possible. It occurred to me that these wealthy folks might have cameras around their property, but I couldn't see any.

I got to the rear of the house, still hidden in the bushes about a hundred feet away, and I saw Eddie struggling to open a ground-floor window.

"Eddie!" I whisper-shouted again. He still did not respond. I made a decision. I bolted out of the bushes—keeping low to the grass—over to the house where Eddie stood, messing with the window. "Eddie! What the fuck are you doing?"

"Doc! Shit! You scared me!"

"What are you doing, Eddie?"

"What's it look like I'm doin', Doc? I'm getting your boy back for you." He looked serious and determined.

I grabbed his arm. "No, Eddie, you can't do this!"

"Doc, I lost my wife and baby, too. And if there was a way to get them back, I would do anything in the world."

"Eddie—"

"This ain't *right*, Doc. Your baby is right inside this house. You gotta get him, Doc. You gotta get him!"

I gulped hard and chills ran through my body. Only minutes before I had been thinking almost the exact same words. Eddie looked so intense I could hardly stand to look at his eyes. He wasn't taking no for an answer.

I looked away and swept the property and the house again for security cameras. I still couldn't see any. When I turned back to Eddie he had his shirt wrapped around the crook of his elbow, and his arm was cocked. He was about to break the window.

"Eddie don't—!" *Crash.* Almost the entire window shattered loudly. I waited for an alarm to sound but none did. Before I could grab him, he was inside.

The window was slightly elevated, and it was more difficult for me to get in than it had been for the longer-legged Eddie. I grabbed the window frame and pulled myself up, careful not to grab hold where any of the jagged glass that remained jutted out from the frame. I wasn't careful enough. A longish shard stabbed into the back of my right arm, just above my elbow. I winced and reached back with my other hand to pull out the shard. It was about two inches long and half an inch wide. It hurt like a bitch. I could feel the blood starting to soak my sleeve and drip down my arm. I held my hand over it tightly to stanch the flow.

I looked around the room I was in, letting my eyes adjust to the dark, which was of a different quality than the dark outside. I was in a large dining room. The table was long and granite and cold-looking. The chairs were black. A chandelier made from the antlers of an animal hung above the table. I looked down and saw that I'd dripped a small puddle of blood onto the rug. *Shit.* I clenched the wound as tightly as I could, but the blood was oozing through my fingers. *Grin and bear it. Gotta get Eddie outta here.*

The house was silent. I watched Eddie quietly disappear around a corner, deeper inside the house. I made it to the spot where he had vanished, and ducked down low to peek around the corner.

Coast clear. No Katie, no Vincent, no maid, no one.

No Eddie, either.

I tiptoed farther into the house, my heart pounding, my head clicking, my teeth grinding.

What the fuck what the fuck what the fuck!?

I didn't like the vibe I was getting. My instincts were telling me to RUN RUN RUN LEAVE LEAVE LEAVE, but I couldn't desert Eddie in there to get busted, or, maybe worse, to snatch the boy from the house. The whole thing felt wrong and ill-planned and destined to end poorly. My brain and my nerves were on fire. My arm throbbed and bled. I lost track of Eddie. The house was large and had many hallways and doorways, and I couldn't determine where he'd gone.

I crept down a long, carpeted hallway, which had three open doors along its walls. I peeked in each of the rooms. The first was an empty office. The second was an empty guest bedroom. The third, another empty bedroom.

There was a staircase at the end of this hallway. I went up, slowly and carefully. The stairs creaked with every step I took, and I cringed. I hadn't heard the creaking before, so maybe Eddie had not gone this way. There didn't seem to be any other route, however, so I proceeded on.

At the top of the stairs was another long hallway. Three more doors. No sign of Eddie. The first door, on the right side of the hallway, was open a crack. I discreetly peeked in. It appeared to be the master bedroom. I couldn't see the whole room through the crack in the door, but I could see some very ornate furniture, and the foot of a prodigious bed. I had no reason to go in there. I crept past the door, silently thankful that the floor was carpeted, making for quieter footfalls.

The next door was a bathroom. Empty. I knew the final door must be the boy's bedroom. My pulse quickened. *Is Eddie in there already?* I leaned my back against the wall and softly banged the back of my head against it, trying to figure out what the heck to do. I was startled when Eddie appeared from the bedroom and said, "Doc—come on."

"Eddie—," I said, grabbing for his arm and missing as he ducked back into the room. I apprehensively followed him in. My heartbeat was thunderous. Eddie stopped a few feet away from the foot of the bed. I stopped right next to him. We both stared down at the bed, where my son slept angelically.

I stared at my perfect child, sleeping soundly before me. My precious little boy, who was taken from his adoring parents, snatched from a perfectly wonderful life, and deluded into believing that these despicable, conniving monsters were his real family.

Decision time.

Could I destroy the world he had come to know? Could I uproot his entire existence? Perhaps the manner in which he arrived here was rendered irrelevant in the face of what would happen to his poor delicate psyche if he were removed from here? *What do I do?*

I heard a creaking noise from the hallway, and my head whipped to the door, which I had partially closed when I'd entered the room. I heard the sound from the hallway again: *creeeeak.*

Someone was coming.

Eddie and I leaped backward against the wall, so that if and when the door opened, we would be behind it, and (hopefully) hidden. I pressed myself as flat as I could against the wall, willing my heart to beat less clamorously. I suddenly realized that our footprints might be visible in the carpeting near the boy's bed, and I began to panic. I stole a glance at the area by craning my neck a bit over the edge of the bed. I didn't see any footprints, but what I saw was much worse: bathed in the dim orange glow of a nightlight by the bed, there were several drops of blood from my arm, dark and obvious, clustered together on the carpet. In addition, there was a trail of little dots that ran from the bed toward the door. I must have blood-dripped my way—Hansel and Gretel–style—all the way from the broken downstairs window right up to my son's bed.

The doorknob jangled, and the door groaned softly as it swung inward. Katie stepped into the room.

CHAPTER
Forty-six

Through the thin sliver of space between the hinge-side of the door and the wall, I saw her enter the room. I carefully peeked around the other side of the door as she quietly walked up to the bed and leaned over to check on the boy. I held my breath. She brushed some hair off of his forehead and kissed him gently. She stood up and looked down at him with a contented little smile.

I didn't dare move.

Satisfied that he was safe and sound, Katie turned to leave the room, but stopped dead when she noticed the spots on the floor next to his bed. She rubbed at the stain with her socked foot. It smudged a bit. I held my breath. If she looked in our direction, she might not see me, as I was completely behind the door. But the much larger Eddie was partially exposed. She would see him.

She bent down and touched the blood with her finger. She looked at her finger, but in the dim light, couldn't determine what the liquid was. She smelled it, but was still uncertain. She looked at the boy, and then she glanced up at the door, right toward Eddie.

My heart stopped.

I expected her to scream.

But she didn't. She looked back down at the floor, and noticed the little dots of blood leading to the bedroom door. *How did she miss Eddie?* She began to follow the trail of dots out the door, and then she was gone.

"We gotta go!" I whispered urgently to Eddie, who nodded vigorously in agreement.

"Hello," came a small voice from the bed.

Startled, I looked down, and my son Jack was sitting up, looking at me.

"H-hi," I whispered. He held up the little blue bear that I'd given him by one of its arms, proudly showing me that he'd kept it. I smiled and whispered, "Cool! I gotta go. Do you want to come with me?"

He shrugged.

I smiled and he did, too. I saw myself in that smile. I knew at that moment we had a bond that no one could break. Here I was, a scary-looking man—the Boogie Man, for all intents and purposes—in his bedroom in the middle of the night, asking him if he wanted to leave with me, and not only wasn't he the least bit afraid, but he was smiling! *He knows the truth! Deep down, he knows!*

I reached out for his hand, and he grabbed mine. "Follow me!" I whispered, and we ran out of the room and into the hallway. I looked to my right, the opposite way from which I'd come, and saw that there was another staircase at the opposite end of the hallway. We headed that way.

After only a few steps an eardrum-bursting scream pierced the silence. It came from somewhere deep in the house. *She followed the trail to the broken window. She knows we're in the house.*

I scooped Jack up into my arms, and when I did, he accidentally dropped the little blue bear onto the carpet. I scooped it up off of the floor and shoved it into my pocket, and then I ran with him as fast as my legs would allow. I caught a glimpse of his face as I barreled down the stairs and he looked scared now.

"What's wrong with my mommy?" he asked.

"It's okay, buddy," I said.

The three of us got to the bottom of the stairs and I heard Katie's terrified howls: "VICTOR! CALL THE PO-LICE! SOMEONE IS IN THE HOUSE!"

I ran hard and fast through the maze of the house. I was disoriented. I lost track of Eddie. I had no idea where I was now and the walls seemed to be closing in on me.

Jack looked terrified, and it hurt my heart.

I got to the end of a long hallway and put Jack down and grabbed his hand. As I turned around to proceed in fleeing I heard a familiar CRACK! and I was instantly thrown into the wall by an unseen force, which slammed hard into my shoulder from behind. I fell to the ground and dropped Jack's hand. I looked at the wall as I fell and saw that it was sprayed with a dark liquid. My entire left arm felt like someone had poured hot lava onto it.

I turned around and saw Victor standing about fifteen feet behind me, a pistol in his hand, pointed at me. Katie scrambled up behind him and shouted, "Joshua!"

My son ran to her.

I glanced down at my shoulder, and saw where the bullet had exited my body in the front. I peered up through pained, squinted eyes to see that I was only feet from the door. I turned and stared back up at them. They were huddled around my son, and Victor only halfheartedly pointed the gun at me now.

I stood up slowly.

"Don't you fucking move!" barked Victor, crazed.

I inched to the door.

"Don't!" he snarled.

I turned and yanked the door open, and just then I heard another CRACK! CRACK! and the wood splintered next to my head and torso.

I bolted into the warm night.

CHAPTER
Forty-seven

I couldn't see Eddie. I assumed he had made it out of the house through some other exit, but I couldn't determine where he'd gone. I ran with all of my might but I couldn't tell how fast I was moving or even if I was running in a straight line. I felt like I was going to pass out at any moment. My shoulder was bleeding an awful lot. I knew if I didn't quickly make it somewhere safe I was done for. The police would be swarming the area any minute.

What am I going to do? Where am I going to go? I'm injured and bleeding and I have nothing and no one. I felt the cold weight of my father's gun in my waistband, and several dark thoughts danced at the corners of my mind. As I neared Sunset Boulevard, a long way still from the beach, I fell to the ground, unable to continue.

As I came to, the sky was getting the slightest bit lighter—from deep blue to purple. I was on the move. Eddie was practically carrying me, my uninjured left arm slung over his wide shoulders. Even with his help, it took a tremendous effort on my part, and I lapsed in and out of consciousness. We finally made it to the beach, and I spotted our tent in the distance. Well, Cecilia's tent, really, but we'd spent the last few nights in it, so it was already starting to feel like home. It was even bigger and better than my old four-man tent that Manny had destroyed. This one was a huge, blue, five-man waterside fortress, and at that moment it looked like an oasis in a great desert. My vision dimmed and dulled, flashed and twinkled. I heard whispers.

Waves. Clicking.

"Hang in there, Doc. We're home," said Eddie, but he sounded like someone else.

He unzipped the tent and I fell inside.

I let the blackness take me again.

I came and went, in and out of the waking world. Minutes or hours passed.

Dark to light.

Here and gone.

I saw Eddie leaning over me. His lips moved but I couldn't hear what he was saying. The sun heated the tent. I was drenched with sweat.

I saw Jack kicking around his soccer ball, heard him laughing.

Ava and I danced. I shivered with fever.

Ava's beautiful hair.

Katie's green eyes and full lips. Music. These are the days of miracle and wonder and don't cry, baby, don't cry, don't cry.

Jack. In his bassinet. There and gone. Tearing through the woods. My hands scratched and bloody. I felt the tears flow.

My father. His gun.

It would be so easy . . .

CHAPTER
Forty-eight

I opened my eyes with a start.

"Doc?" A woman's voice said my name outside of the tent.

"Ava?" I asked softly through a very dry throat and mouth. *How could this be?*

I looked around. No sign of Eddie.

The zipper on the tent's door flap began to move of its own accord.

"Can I come in?"

The flap fell open.

A woman was silhouetted by sunlight. When she leaned into the tent I could see her worried face.

Cecilia.

Not Ava. Cecilia. I felt weak and delirious and silly for believing that it could've been Ava.

"Oh God, Doc," she cried. "Oh God oh God."

"I'm okay," I croaked.

"No, Doc. You're soaked with blood! We have to get you to a hospital!" She grabbed a T-shirt from a corner of the tent and wrapped it around my arm as a tourniquet— something I should have done as soon as I was injured.

Some doctor you are.

"Doc, you broke into their house?! You tried to kidnap their child?! It's all over the television! Why did you do that, Doc?! How could you do that?!"

My child, I wanted to say. I couldn't muster the strength for a proper response. I just shook my head.

"You're in trouble, Doc. I told you not to do anything like this . . ."

"How'd you find me?" I asked.

"The tent." She was crying.

I was vaguely aware of shadows surrounding the tent. Silhouettes dancing behind the blue vinyl. I couldn't figure out what was real.

"Cecilia, what's—"

"I'm sorry, Doc. I'm so sorry."

CHAPTER
Forty-nine

The shadows were real. They surrounded the tent on all sides. From the great wide beyond, a gravelly, no-nonsense voice squawked, "PLEASE EXIT THE TENT WITH YOUR HANDS IN THE AIR."

I was not processing the situation properly. I could not move or get up even if I'd wanted to. I was on complete information overload.

My brain was malfunctioning.

I thought of my father's gun again. I reached for it with my good arm. I could hear them outside the tent, yelling, but I could no longer understand what they were saying. The one voice had multiplied into many—a veritable chorus—pleading, begging, ordering me to come out. The CLICKing had returned with a vengeance, full volume. It wasn't even a click anymore. It was the sound of a motor roaring. It was the loudest drumbeat in the world. It filled my head and made me see stars. My vision was strange and hallucinatory. Every image left a trail behind it. Every movement blurred and distorted my perspective further.

I felt the handle of the gun at my waist.

I thought about my father.

And then something sliced through the tent fabric and the sun blinded me.

There were hands all over me. They grabbed at me and pulled me out of the tent, onto warm sand. Pain seared through my body, exploding in my brain like fireworks.

"Please!" I thought I heard Cecilia say. "Please don't hurt him!"

I tried to scream but I simply could not. I was trapped in my mind. My body would simply not respond to my brain's commands.

They flipped me onto my stomach and held my head down. They pulled my arms behind my back. My vision seared a hot white. That's all I remember.

CHAPTER

Fifty

I woke up in a bed.

When I opened my eyes I could not believe where I was.

Not possible.

I blinked a few times to clear my vision. It didn't work.

Everything was fuzzy and indistinct, my eyelids heavy.

I turned my head on the pillow, and vaguely saw what appeared to be Jack's little blue teddy bear sitting on the nightstand next to the bed, before I surrendered back into a dreamless sleep.

I awoke in the same room.

How did I get here? This doesn't make sense.

I attempted to rub my eyes with the heels of my palms, but found that my left wrist was handcuffed to the bed, and my right wrist was attached to an IV drip.

I surveyed my surroundings again. The room looked almost exactly the same as I remembered, aside from the fact that the large comfortable bed that I'd once spent so much time in had been replaced by a hospital bed.

I was in my hotel room at Shutters on the Beach.

What the hell is going on?

I tried to call out for help, but my voice was hoarse and raspy. I leaned over for a cup of ice water that sat on a tray next to my bed, a blue bendy straw protruding from its lip. I sipped from the straw, and I could feel the cold liquid winding its way through my insides, all the way down to my stomach.

"Help!" I shouted weakly.

Nothing.

"Hello? Help!"

No response.

I looked to my left, behind my head. It wasn't just an IV attached to me. There was a whole mess of wires attaching me to machines that were keeping track of my vitals. A huge bandage was wrapped around my torso and shoulder, and another around my elbow.

Did all of that really happen? Now what? Where is Cecilia? The cops? How did I end up back in a suite at one of the most expensive hotels in Santa Monica?

My thoughts were still sluggish. My body weak and not fully cooperative.

Whoever connected all this crap to me must be monitoring me somehow.

I looked around for some kind of call button, but could not locate one. "Help!" I tried again. "Someone help me!" I felt myself getting very agitated, very quickly.

Panicky.

"Help! Please!"

I heard the beep beep beep of the heart monitor speed up to beepbeepbeep.

"Hello?"

I was startled when someone in the room said, "Shh-hhh."

I whipped my head around and was startled to find that Eddie was sitting in a corner of the room in a chair. I hadn't noticed him before. He had his finger to his lips.

"Eddie! What are you doing here? What is happening?"

"Don't yell, Doc. Just take it easy," he said.

And then my attention swung back to the door as the doorknob CLANKED. I stared at it.

It appeared that the locking mechanism had been removed from the inside of the door. I was locked into this room. *What the fuck?*

"Why are we locked in here, Eddie?"

He didn't have time to answer before the doorknob jangled some more and I heard the dead bolt disengage.

The door swung open and Charlie Walter walked into my room wearing a white lab coat and holding a clipboard in his hand.

He closed the door and walked over to the foot of my bed. "Hey, you're awake," he said through his mustache.

I looked at Eddie, who was standing now in a sort

of defensive posture, like he needed to protect me from Charlie. Charlie did not acknowledge his presence. I couldn't speak. I didn't know what was real anymore! How could Eddie and I be in my old hotel room? And why were we locked in? Now Charlie Walter was here, dressed like a doctor and carrying a clipboard?

"Been a long time," Charlie said softly. I stared at him, speechless. "You're all over the news, you know."

I looked down at my handcuffs and my bandages in response. "We're not letting you out so quick this time," he said.

I stared at him but could not summon any words. When our stare got too awkward he looked down at his clipboard. "How are you feeling today? Your vitals look good. Dr. Lerer will be in to check your sutures."

I didn't respond.

"You must be pretty groggy still, so I'll leave you alone for now. But maybe you'll be up for a conversation soon?"

I didn't respond.

He pursed his lips, nodded resignedly, and turned to leave.

"Wait," I said. He turned around. "I'm sorry. I just don't . . . I'm confused right now."

"That's perfectly natural."

I looked at his lab coat. "Last time I saw you . . ." I gulped hard again, looked down and shook my head. "I mean . . . aren't you my lawyer?"

"No, Bobby. I'm your doctor."

"But I remember so clearly, the last time I was here—"

"Last time you were here you were in a chemically in-
duced stupor for almost the entire length of your stay. Do
you want to tell me exactly what you remember?"

I wanted so badly to run my hand through my hair
or rub my face, but I couldn't because both of my hands
were shackled in one way or another. A nurse walked
into the room to change my IV bag. I recognized her. She
was one of the little Mexican maids I'd known from my
last stay here. Why was she dressed as a nurse now? My
brain continued to spin like a globe. This whole situation
was a complete mind-fuck. All of my facts were slippery. I
wanted to answer him, but I couldn't nail anything down.
"I think I've lost my mind, Charlie."

"Charlie?" he asked.

"Yeah . . . Ch-Charlie. Charlie Walter."

"My name is Dr. Jeffrey Stein, Bobby."

"But—last time—"

"It's okay, Bobby. You're just a little confused right
now. You're okay, though. You're safe here."

"Why am I in this hotel room? Why are we locked in?"

"This isn't a hotel room. It's a psychiatric hospital."

I looked around the room again, and he was right.
The room had changed suddenly. No more hotel room.

I was in a small, cell-like hospital room.

Aw, fuck.

I started to panic. "What's going on here?"

"Like I said, it's perfectly normal for you to be confused. You've had a major psychotic event."

"If I'm in a cell in a psychiatric hospital, then why

is Eddie locked in here with me?" I asked, throwing a thumb in Eddie's direction.

Dr. Stein's eyes followed my thumb, but didn't properly land on Eddie. He scribbled something on his clipboard.

"What are you writing?"

He inhaled and exhaled and looked at me sympathetically. "Bobby, there is no one in this room except for the two of us."

He was right. When I looked over at Eddie, he was gone, too. Just like the hotel room.

Oh, you gotta be shittin' me.

My mind went back to the night in Katie's house when she had looked right at Eddie, but didn't see him. And then I thought about what Ava had said when I'd visited her. She said that they'd seen me walking the streets alone talking to myself. But I almost never walked anywhere without Eddie.

I closed my eyes and tried to summon memories of my recent past. I needed to reexamine them through this new lens.

I thought about my little doggy friend Bob Barker. I pictured us in the parking lot at my office. In my car. The two of us sitting on the couch at my house. But then my memories transformed. Bob Barker vanished from them. And I was alone—in the parking lot, in the car, on the couch—talking to the spot where the dog had been a moment before.

Then I saw myself and Eddie walking down the beach, talking to each other like we'd done so many times over the years. And then Eddie vanished. And it was me, alone, talking to the spot where Eddie had just been. Talking to no one.

Then Eddie and I were on that bench, watching the sun rise. And then Eddie vanished. Then I saw Eddie breaking into Katie's house, which morphed into *me* breaking their window with my own elbow. And then I saw myself throwing all of my possessions into the fire on the beach. My tent. My sleeping bag. My suitcase. Everything except for my father's manuscript. Not Manny. *Me.* And then I ran down the beach, terrified, as it burned.

I opened my eyes, panicked.

"What is happening to me, Doctor?"

"Bobby, you suffer from paranoid schizophrenia, which manifests itself through delusions, hallucinations, and various other forms of social dysfunction. We believe that this illness—from all you've told us over your time as our patient—was brought on by a serious trauma you experienced, probably the suicide of your father. Of course, it also has genetic roots, and excessive drug and alcohol use only exacerbated your condition."

"You said delusions. Delusions about what?"

"I don't know, exactly, Bobby. But for example, you and I have interacted many times over the years in a doctor-patient relationship. Yet, you believed just now—probably from very real memories that you have—that I was your attorney rather than your physician. Also, in the past, when you've been a patient here, you've told us that your name was Nathan Vacario."

"No. What? I don't remember that. How is that *possible?*"

"It was also likely a delusion which led you to break into the home of a stranger last night."

"No, Doctor. That was not a delusion! They aren't strangers! I know it's hard to believe, but that story is true!"

"Well, that's the thing about delusions, Bobby. The very psychiatric definition of 'delusion' in the *Diagnostic and Statistical Manual of Mental Disorders* is 'A false belief based on incorrect inference about external reality that is firmly sustained despite what almost everyone else believes and despite what constitutes incontrovertible and obvious proof or evidence to the contrary. The belief is not one ordinarily accepted by other members of the person's culture or subculture.' Do you understand that definition, Bobby?"

"Yes, Dr. Stein. I understand that definition. I was a doctor, too, remember?"

Dr. Stein raised an eyebrow and bobbed his head back and forth a little bit, in a way that implied that what I'd just said might not be true.

"What? What are you saying? That I *wasn't* a doctor? That my whole entire life story is . . . what? Made up? Invented? By a crazy person?" Ava's words echoed in my brain.

"No, I'm not saying your *whole* story is a product of your illness—a sheer fabrication—but I am saying that *much* of it probably is comprised of delusion, and that once we get your illness under control, which I am confident we will, it is going to take you quite some time to piece together the fact from the fiction."

All I could manage to say was, "No," but my mind

reeled. I knew that what Dr. Stein was saying had some validity. I knew that my mind had been anything but healthy since Jack disappeared and my life fell apart all those years ago. The constant clicking sounds in my head, the paranoia . . . but how could Eddie have never even existed? How could that possibly be? Could I have completely invented Bob Barker and Manny as well? What else was in my imagination? Did I ever even stay in a hotel? Was I blending my memories or were my memories pure concoctions? What was real and what was invented by my sick mind? How could I know for sure that this conversation I was having with the doctor was real?

One thing was for certain: I was not willing, no matter what this guy said, to entertain the idea that my life prior to my son's disappearance was not 100 percent fact. I could not have created my whole life with Ava, my time with Dicky, my baby boy. But what about this whole thing with Katie and Jack? It certainly seemed crazy. Could it all be a delusion?

No. I know it's real.

But then a little voice of reason in the back of my mind whispered, *You were sure Eddie was real, too.*

My heart began to break.

CHAPTER

Fifty-one

I spent the next few days trying to sort through the details of my life. Trying to separate fact from fiction with the help of Dr. Jeffrey Stein.

The drugs helped, too.

Dr. Stein was able to clear up one thing—he explained that the clicking in my head was a perfectly normal symptom of schizophrenia. He asked what the sound reminded me of. I told him it sounded like tap dancing, or someone pounding on a typewriter. He jotted some notes about that. I didn't get many more answers from him. He was unable to confirm that I'd been married to a woman named Ava. He didn't know anything about my missing son, or that I'd been a pediatrician. Yet, Dicky had told me that they'd visited me when I was in the hospital. I didn't know what he was talking about then, but it made sense now. But if they'd visited me here, wouldn't they have told the doctors all about my past and what had caused me to lose my mind? Dr. Stein didn't recall their visits. I was confused.

How can I determine what is real when everything seems real? It's nearly impossible to grasp on to anything. There's no yardstick. No reference points. No proof! In my mind—in my memory—everything had equal veri-similitude, so how could I possibly determine what was authentic? Everything in my life might or might not be the product of my imagination! It was maddening! I started second guessing that I'd ever *had* that conversation at Ava and Dicky's house. If Eddie didn't exist, shit, who's to say that Dicky did? The more I obsessed about it all, the more bewildered and distressed it made me.

After a few days of this I was wallowing in despair. I was medicated and confused and dispirited.

And then Dr. Jeffrey Stein figured it all out.

When I opened my eyes, there he was—standing at the foot of my bed, a folder and a large stack of paper in his hands, looking anxious.

"Bobby? You awake?" he asked.

I stared, wondering if he was a figment of my imagination.

"I don't know anymore," I said.

"I want to talk to you, Bobby."

"Okay."

"Are you up for a conversation? Can you sit up?"

Dr. Stein moved to the side of my bed and pressed the button to raise the back. He looked very serious.

"Bobby, I want you to tell me your entire story. Start at the beginning. I want to hear everything."

"Everything?"

"From as early as you can remember."

"Haven't we been through this? What does it matter?"

"I think I've got some answers for you. But first I need to hear you tell me your story exactly as you recall it."

I was so tired. So sick of not knowing what was what. Tired of searching for answers and having no one come to my rescue.

"Trust me, Bobby. Please."

So I did. I told Dr. Stein the entire story from the very beginning. All about my childhood, my father's novel and his suicide. How Ava and I met, got married. How I started my practice with Dicky and how it was so successful. How Ava and I had a baby. How Katie Turner reappeared in my life after so many years. How we took her in and all the strife that caused. The kiss and the tragedy of Jack's disappearance. How it destroyed my marriage and led to my downfall. My drinking and drugging. My time in the hotel and then my time on the street. My attempted suicide, and meeting Eddie. Katie's reemergence as Kerri Taylor. My suspicions and then confirmation that she and Vincent stole my son. I told him about Charlie Walter and the Mexican maids and Karyn Shelly and Manny and Cecilia. I told him about the break-in and how the cops arrested me on the beach and how I woke up here.

When I was finished, Dr. Stein had a strange look on his face. It was a look of restrained astonishment. A look that said he knew something. Something vital.

"Do you recognize this, Bobby?" he asked, as he pulled something from the stack of papers on his lap. He held it up for me to see. It was my father's manuscript, *The Human Being*.

"Yes, of course," I said. "My father's novel."

"It was found in your tent when you were arrested. It was checked in here as one of your few possessions. I went back through the records from the last time you were here, which was almost six years ago, and this was among your possessions then, too."

"Yeah? So?"

"So, in an effort to help you piece together your past, I went through your stuff, and when I found this, I had a look."

As soon as he said those words I started feeling odd. I can't describe the feeling, except to say that I could feel my face getting flushed and my nerves revving.

"And?" I asked, wishing he would just get to the point.

"I ended up reading the whole book, Bobby. And . . . I don't know how to say this . . . but the story you just told me about your life . . . just about every detail . . . is the exact story that your father wrote in this book."

CHAPTER
Fifty-two

I felt the floor go out from under me. I mean I really felt like I was falling down a hole.

"Wh-what?"

CLICKCLICKCLICK . . .

"Your story. It isn't *your* story. You've inserted yourself into the story from this manuscript, *The Human Being*. You introduced many of your own details, like September 11th, for instance, which obviously your father couldn't have written about, but for the most part, everything you just told me came straight from your father's novel. The main character in your father's book is named Nathan Vacario, and all of those people that you told me about in the story of your life, those are *all* characters in this manuscript. Ava, Dicky, Jack, Katie Turner, Charlie Walter . . . *everyone*."

"No," was all I could muster. I felt the tears

welling up now. CLICKCLACKCLICKCLACKCLICK-CLACK . . . rapid fire. "No! That's impossible! I've never even read it!"

"You have read it. You don't remember reading it, but clearly you read it at some point, and a part of you knows it well."

"No . . ." I flashed to an image of Eddie reading the manuscript. And Manny, too. And that random homeless woman on the street.

"Your father's manuscript ended more or less where your story ends. The main character becomes convinced that he knows who kidnapped his child, but is unable to prove it because of the circumstances of his current life as a homeless man."

"This doesn't make any sense!"

"It does make sense, Bobby. Your father's suicide had a profound effect on your young mind. It's not at all surprising that you developed an obsession with the thing that caused his death. And when he left you his manuscript in his will—almost, as you put it, like a challenge to finish it—I believe that created this very powerful compulsion in your mind. The need to finish your father's story and figure out the ending."

"It's not possible that I imagined it all! If it's not real then what have I been doing all this time?"

"You've been in and out of hospitals and institutions and living on the streets for a very long time. I can't surmise any other actual details of your life aside from that."

I was desperate to grab on to something as I fell and fell and fell, but there was nothing except for the incessant clicking. CLICK CLICK CLICK . . . and then, after the clicking, a new sound . . . **DING!**

This high-pitched bell rang out like a gunshot in my mind. This was an entirely unfamiliar sound in my head. A coda to this clicking I'd been hearing for so long.

When I heard the DING I knew what the clicking sound in my mind was. What it had been all along: it was the sound of my father typing. The sound I heard through the wall for so many years when I was a child. The sound I fell asleep to every single night of my life up until my father died. It was the sound of his steady decline into madness. And it was mine as well.

I was like a derailed train.

Images from my many years on the streets and in various hospitals assaulted my brain like lightning strikes. I didn't want to hear any more. I closed my eyes and since I couldn't cover my ears I started to scream and I just couldn't stop. I was handcuffed to the bed still, but I bucked and kicked and flailed and felt the IV needles tear out of my arms. Dr. Stein backed away and hit a button by the door that would summon the nurses. I heard him say something urgently into the speaker on the wall as I continued to freak out. The door burst open and people in scrubs came rushing in to subdue me. Three of them held me down and one of them injected me with something. I immediately felt the medication take hold. "It can't be true," I heard myself say. As I let the sedative take over, I saw a mental picture of me and Ava and Jack. I was holding baby Jack up in the air and spinning around and he was smiling. Ava was watching and laughing beside me. And then nothing.

CHAPTER

Fifty-three

I woke up staring, once again, at the little blue teddy bear on my nightstand, which sat there staring back at me with its tiny, black, beady eyes. I blinked a few times, trying to clear the fuzziness of the sedation from my eyes. I remembered what the doctor had told me earlier and my heart sank. I simply could not accept the idea that I was a crazy man who had borrowed my whole life story from the pages of a book written by my insane father. As I stared at the bear, I thought about my life. *How could it all be imaginary? If that bear didn't belong to my son, Jack, then where did it come from? Where does the real stuff end and the imagined begin?* I'd spent so many years carrying this bear around with me. Smelling it. Holding it. Drying my tears with it. It had been the only concrete token that I'd had left of this supposed child of mine. A gossamer thread holding us together.

I don't want to believe this.

"Help me," I said to the bear. Thankfully, the bear didn't answer.

Not with words anyway.

But something *did* happen as I stared at that little blue bear.

A gossamer thread holding us together.

Wrapped tightly around the bear's arm, so thin, so delicate, almost transparent, was a tiny blond hair. I flashed back to the boy in the house that I broke into. My boy, Jack. Holding this bear. His beautiful blond hair just like Ava's. I felt a surge of hopefulness. I heard a familiar chuckle, and I turned to my other side. Eddie was sitting in the chair in the corner.

He was smiling from ear to ear.

"There's your proof," Eddie said.

"What?"

"Have 'em test the hair, Doc. They'll see he's your son. They'll see you didn't make it all up!"

I looked back at the bear, and then back to Eddie. *Maybe he's onto something . . .*

"That's a good idea, Eddie!"

"Hell yeah!" he said. "Don't believe that doctor. He just wants to keep you here! There's no way your whole life ain't real. The doctor said it himself—your dad couldn't've written bout 9/11 cuz that shit didn't even happen yet when he wrote his book! That's proof right there that this is all BS!"

I whipped my head back to the bear. The hair was still there, tied around the bear's arm.

"I really think you're onto something, Eddie!" I said.

"We'll make this right, Doc."

"Yeah, we will," I said to my boy Eddie. I smiled and began to formulate a new plan to get the hell outta there.

Acknowledgments

Many thanks to my agents, Jud Laghi at LJK Literary and Shari Smiley at CAA.

Tremendous gratitude to everyone at Simon & Schuster who played a part in bringing this book to fruition, but especially: David Rosenthal, Aileen Boyle, Leah Wasielewski, Nina Pajak, Kimberly Cowser, Jackie Seow, Kate Ankofski, and, of course, the brilliant Kerri Kolen Fox.

All you need is love, and I'm blessed beyond merit in that department. To that end:

Thank you to my father, Steve Rotter—smartest guy I know.

Thank you to my mother, Karyn Rotter—love, personified.

Thank you to my wife, Bree. You are beautiful in every way. I consider myself the luckiest guy in the world to have you to spend my life with. You are also quite lucky.

Thank you to my amazing sisters, Emily and Julie, and my bro-in-law Ben Lerer—BFFs.

Thank you to my wonderful parents-in-law, Lewis and Lynar Abel—cherished sages.

Thank you to my dearest friends and family— whether it's as readers, listeners, idea bounce-boards, sanity-givers, or simply as drinking cohorts, I can't do this without you: Greg and Mel Walter, Jordan Young, Marc Stenzler, Tobias Levine, Doug Finkel, Mike and Julie Davis, Coulter Mcabery, Brian Sapp, Tom Hess, Jamil Downey, Eric Roach, Christine Alvarez, Matt Collar, Ashley Fox, Liz Marks, Josh Weisman, Richard and Ruth Wiggs, Ceil Rotter, Lori Farbanish Rotter, Bryan Denberg, Chris and Dori Carter, Sonia Scheideman, Erin Beck, and Johnnie Walker. Also Thom Yorke, Trey Anastasio, and James Mercer for your essential company while I wrote this one.

Thank you to all the fans who took the time to write such kind emails to me about my first book, *Duck Duck Wally*. Writing a novel is a pain in the ass–your warm appreciation makes it all worth it.

See you next time.
Much love.

Gabe Rotter
Santa Monica, California
May, 2010

Printed in the United States
By Bookmasters